MYTHS, LIES, and NONSENSE

ROGER COLE

ISBN
979-8-88945-116-7 (Paperback)
979-8-88945-117-4 (Ebook)

Brilliant Books Literary
137 Forest Park Lane Thomasville
North Carolina 27360 USA

Table of Contents

About the Author

I have no credentials to establish me as an expert in any of the social science disciplines but then this book is not a study in human behavior, it is an exposition about the verbal and visual cues that limit our choices; an exposé of the myths, lies and nonsense that surround us. Thus, to write such a book does not require credentials, it requires experience – you know, been there and done that – and the perspective only gained by having been on the planet a long, long time.

I've worked some fun and interesting jobs like job coach for mentally challenged people, waiter, bartender, checkout clerk as well as a manager in a large corporation, negotiator for billion-dollar contracts and team member for some astonishing engineering advancements. I have served in the military, protested against wars I determined were unjust and worked in military programs requiring Top Secret, Special Access clearances.

Contradictory?

Perhaps.

In addition to a diverse series of jobs, I have lived on three continents, visited more than twenty countries and learned that in spite of the cultural differences that give each city or region a pulse, a vibrancy that is unique, there is a common thread of community that exists solely because we are human; that almost everyone would rather laugh and play than be angry; that love and lust, although sometimes indistinguishable, know no imaginary political boundaries; that communication depends as much on gestures and body language as it does on words and that understanding comes more from impression than analysis.

I have laughed, loved, hated, been consumed by anger and wallowed in lust but I have been steadfast in my love for my wife of over forty years.

Those are the credentials of living and the diversity of my life qualifies me as an expert on society's myths, lies and nonsense.

One

What's Up?

Last Tuesday you woke up and eventually got to the point that you looked in the mirror to begin the task of applying makeup.

You're running a little late and might have thought: "Why the hell am I doing this?"

Or you might decide to skip the eyeliner but remembered how sharp Marcia always looks.

"Marcia, Marcia, Marcia – Bitch!"

That's the way it goes, sports fans. You are doing something that you may or may not like but you have to because you are a woman and if you don't you might get ridiculed, harassed or worse.

When you were a child, dressing up was fun. It still is until you have to do it every day.

As you grew older you noticed that your brother got away with things but "boys will be boys" and you were "such a pretty little girl".

The trivialization had begun!

Eventually, you couldn't even walk down the street without being harassed.

In 1998 Maggie Hadleigh-West created a documentary entitled *War Zone* in which she depicted the hazards and harassment that women faced solely for walking the streets. In the subsequent sixteen years there have been various YouTube productions on the same subject and the harassment of the walking women is virtually unchanged.

I bring this up because the Civil Rights Act was passed along with subsequent amendments and legal clarifications about sexual harassment decades before Ms. Hadleigh-West's documentary and you would think that since sexual harassment is basically illegal, men's harassment of women walking the streets or anywhere else would have subsided.

It has not.

It is true that sexual harassment and discrimination has diminished somewhat in the specific areas covered by the laws but that is because brave women have spoken up or sued but that hasn't removed the prejudice.

So it seems that there are two types of sexual harassment. One is the type that is defined by law or tort law. These rules mainly cover employment or working conditions and grievances are handled through the courts or the media. It's a serious pain in the ass, but it can be handled.

Most of the harassment women endure is not prosecutable and falls into the category of casual sexism. You know what I mean, catcalls, inappropriate touching, being called "honey" or "sweetheart" stuff like that. Definitely stupid and very annoying but there isn't a whole lot you can do about it without causing a scene which will probably get you nowhere.

Not good, but that junk is just the surface manifestations of casual sexism. It's actually much worse and hugely more insidious and damaging.

Sexism, casual or otherwise, has very little to do with you, the individual, it has to do with power and the projection thereof. That's hard to swallow when you're walking down the street and some dufus is making comments about your derriere but it's true because he's letting you know that he has control of the situation and you can't do anything about it. All prejudices are that way. They are based on a single or a set of premises that are false. Racial prejudice is based on the assumption that the color of a person's skin determines their character. Thus a person of white skin might be determined to be privileged and perhaps evil and not to be trusted regardless of any evidence to the contrary.

The prejudice against women is worse than other prejudices because it transcends race, class, economic status, age and any other grouping you can think of. It is based on the misconception that a woman's sole function is to breed and provide sexual pleasures for men and, you know what, nobody says that but almost everyone believes it!

For centuries women all over the world have been taught that they are incomplete without a husband and that the most glorious thing you can do is bear children. What a crock! In the 21st century we don't need more children we need less!

All prejudices stem from ancient, invalid sets of rules that almost everyone accepts as true even in the face of all information to the contrary. Casual sexism is just like that, it's based on a bunch of pseudo rules that have, in one way or another, been around for centuries and their purpose is to make every woman on the planet not OK.

"Let me take care of you baby."

Sounds a little vague and that is exactly the problem.

When we think of rules we think of laws, regulations or even etiquette and that's fine because they are written down someplace and if we don't like them they can be changed to conform to current standards or practices – for the most part. Pseudo rules on the other hand aren't written down anywhere, don't have the force of law, change over time and are arbitrary and capricious.

Fashion rules leap to mind.

You know what I mean. Some things were alright a few years ago and no longer are or don't matter. Stuff like matching accessories, black and brown together, no white after Labor Day, hip hugger pants, etc., etc.

There are also rules about age, weight, height, and comportment in general.

You may have noticed that all of these rules have nothing whatsoever to do with who you are; rather they have to do with an image you might want or are required to project but it is a double whammy because there are rules defining the image itself.

Confused?

That's the whole point.

Keep women confused and then they can be mastered.

A powerful woman, say a legislator or a lawyer or CEO makes an important point on some issue and almost invariably there will be comments on her attire or demeanor and suddenly her message is trivialized.

"I liked what she said but did you notice that she was wearing flats?"

Wrong shoes, ergo wrong idea.

At this point you might think that there is some kind of a conspiracy going on and there is – sort of.

I say "sort of" because the conspiracy isn't planned or even organized but it is the result of thousands of years of female subjugation that has become second nature to almost everyone on the planet, male or female

The fact is that women are almost always under attack. No matter how much "progress" is made there seems to be an undercurrent of prejudice against women that says, basically, that they are not good enough. The prejudice permeates the entire society at all levels and, amazingly, some women are afflicted with this prejudice as well.

Did/do plumbers, electricians, etc. treat women differently than men?

Almost universally.

Were/are women paid less?

Almost universally.

Are women subjected to stares and subtle harassment or casual sexism?

Almost every day.

Etc.

Women get beat up about all sorts of things and the attacks don't make any sense.

For a long time I couldn't figure out why.

As far as I could see, except for physical configuration, all of my women friends and men friends were/are pretty much alike. Some smart, some dumb, some fun, some boring, some ambitious, some not so much, etc. so what is it about women that elicits disrespect?

I have talked to women all over the world about this and the answer slowly became clear.

The prejudice against women is based on a very simple, universally accepted concept: men are masculine and women are feminine.

Let me say that again.

The prejudice against women is based on a very simple, universally accepted concept: men are masculine and women are feminine.

Think about that for a minute.

What does it mean?

You kind of have an idea but you don't really know with absolute certainty.

You may know biologically or in terms of physical configuration but socially…?

There seems to be some sort of rule that states that if you are configured as male or female you must behave a certain way – mostly. I say mostly because some of the behaviors or traits we generally associate with men, like athletic or competitive, can also apply to some women and conversely some behaviors like compassionate or sensitive, usually associated with women, can also apply to some men.

Very confusing.

It seems that even though we can't define what femininity or masculinity is as a specifically defined state, we do have a sense, a feeling if you will, of what they mean and spend a great deal of time and effort to try to conform to what we think the feeling tells us.

One of the feelings the vast majority of people (both genders) have is that femininity is somehow not as good as masculinity and that translates into women being somehow inferior.

How dumb is that?

Of course in the "good old days", that superior/inferior idea was pretty much accepted and very few people thought about it much. Femininity for single women meant being cheerful, childlike, soft spoken, demure, shy, alluring, attractive and other stuff while for married women it meant gladly bearing children, caring for and submitting to your man, household chores, raising the children and little else. Masculinity pretty much meant macho – period.

Finally in the 1960s, hundreds of years of struggle to overcome the superior/inferior thing came to a head and good laws were passed dictating the abolishment of gender inequality but laws don't change people's feelings much and the problem persists.

For example, from the sixties to now, the concept of what it means to be masculine has not changed much. There have been a few tweaks in terms of displaying emotion, parenting and some jobs but still pretty much the same.

For women however, the changes have been more substantial. The list of changes is long but here are four biggies: women now have financial control over their lives, they have assumed jobs that used to be forbidden, they are a political and economic force and some are hugely admired political, financial and sports personalities.

Big changes and pretty much screwed up the old concept of femininity except for the superficial. A woman may be a single mother juggling a job as, say, a police officer and a parent (mother and father) but wants to feel feminine while doing it. Obviously it's pretty near impossible to feel feminine while busting some burglar or trying to fix a leaky faucet or whatever, so her only recourse is to try and look the part. As soon as that happens, those who view her put her in a box (maybe she does as well) and the person she actually is – strong, mother, father, plumber, etc. – is overlooked.

"Wow, Officer Miller, you clean up really well!"

Casual sexism at work.

The presumption being that if she looks the part she must be that way.

There is nothing inherently wrong with that presumption except it is a little disconnected from reality because every woman is by definition feminine regardless of how she adorns herself. Thus, the concept, the idea, of what feminine is and what it is not must be something other than looks alone.

It seems that we are all in some sort of a box.

Obviously people react to each other based on their appearance but for women the situation is much worse than for men. Take sports figures for instance. I could name any number but think of Danica Patric (NASCAR driver) or Maryeve Dufault (Motorcycle racer who earned money for her bikes by modeling). Would an auto mechanic that didn't know who these women are treat them differently than a man?

Probably, because in his mind a lovely lady can't possibly know anything about cars.

Too bad for him.

This distinction in treatment occurs all over the place. Anecdotal evidence suggests that "pretty" women get favorable treatment in the workplace, powerful intelligent women are called pushy and dissed for their choices of hairstyle or clothes, much of the media depersonalizes and objectifies women from all walks of life, etc.

I'm sure you can cite examples of your own

We all know that this reality – complicated, confusing, pervasive and unfair – is wrong but put up with it anyhow.

Why?

Because from the day you were born you were paraded about in pink attire signifying that you were a girl child. Who invented this concept is unknown and as far as anyone can tell the idea of pink for girls and blue for boys wasn't a hard over rule until the late 1940's and early 1950's which, incidentally, coincides with the development of mass marketing and the birth of the Feminine Industrial Complex.

The Feminine Industrial Complex "exists" much like the Military Industrial Complex "exists". That is that it is an amalgam of industries and organizations who's focus is women. In my mind, it is comprised of two groups. The first group is those industries that manufacture, distribute and publicize "beauty" products and services. Also included are written material from the ridiculous like the *National Enquirer* and *US* to the sublime like *Vogue, Elle* and *Men Are from Mars, Women Are from Venus* (maybe that one is ridiculous as well). The principal message of these members of the Complex is that you, woman, have minimal value but if you buy our products your value will increase. They also insist that the use of their products – makeup, clothes, etc. – will define your femininity and you will be glorious. Who you really are is of no interest to them.

The second group is the medical, political and religious establishments and their products are ideas about the correct place and position of a woman in society. Their idea of femininity revolves around insisting that a woman always be ready to breed. Contraception, abortion and even heavy physical or intellectual work are no-nos. They also foster some kind of concept about the "proper" appearance and behavior of women more in line with the pre-1960's idea of femininity.

Unfortunately the second group has the power to enact laws to institutionalize their bigotry. Since the beginning of the 21st century over 300 laws have been passed throughout the United States negatively affecting a woman's reproductive choices and female specific health; the Supreme Court of the United States has issued a ruling that the sensibilities of a corporation are more important than a woman's access to medication and there is a growing movement that takes the position that a fertilized human egg is a person and thus entitled to all the rights and benefits of a citizen. This means that if a woman miscarries she may have committed murder and is subject to investigation. Currently there have been about 200 women have been investigated and some have been incarcerated for miscarrying even though they may not have known that they were pregnant.

This is not good.

Anyhow, the combined result of the efforts of the Complex is to define what feminine is and exert huge pressure for all women to conform to their definition.

Naturally there is a lot of confusion.

Members of the first group are all competing with each other to maximize their profits and are constantly changing things around so that no consumer ever knows what is correct. Members of the second group are also in competition and are falling all over each other to show which one of them is more protective of their idea of social values which includes their definition of femininity.

That's why women put up with a reality that is complicated, confusing, pervasive and unfair; the pressure to conform is intense and they really have nowhere to turn.

You are a woman and you probably have a pretty good idea of who you are but you must conform to the Complex's idea of femininity or face harassment, ridicule or worse. Besides, the products produced are generally beneficial, fun and often make you feel good. Unfortunately the message of the Complex is often demeaning, intrusive and insensitive.

They ignore the fact that a woman is a woman; an individual with a unique brain, with passion, compassion, intelligence, drive, ambition, strength and the thousands of other attributes that make a human being. She also has faults, insecurities, makes mistakes and sometimes just tries to shrug it off as best she can – like the rest of humanity. In addition, a woman is feminine by definition regardless of whatever anyone else thinks.

The disconnect between what we are taught is feminine and the reality of this century is palpable. The definition of femininity offered by the Complex is vague by design to keep women on the defensive and to neutralize her power and steal her money.

This nonsense has to stop.

The old ideas of femininity and masculinity are myths that have no meaning in the 21ˢᵗ century and should be eliminated from our minds and lexicon.

The first step is to neutralize the power of the Complex and make them work for you to allow you to be you instead of allowing them to dictate their ideas. To do that, you must know what the rules are and how they work.

I can show you that but only you can fix them.

Two

Do You See What I'm Saying?

Fewer assaults are more vigorous than the presumption that one's weight is related to one's worth. It's a shame actually because the extreme efforts put forth to fit into the caricature created by the Complex are really not necessary and tends to subvert every person's natural optimism.

The whole subject of eating conjures up weight, dieting, nutrition and a whole bunch of other related topics. All this stuff has been hashed and rehashed to death and frankly it's…

Boring!

Sometimes I feel that if I see another weight-loss advertisement, I'm going to puke. Interestingly enough, those ads are usually sandwiched between commercials about food (sorry about the pun). I have no idea if what I said about the sequence of the ads is true, but it sure seems like it. The sequence goes like this: eat (ad about snacks, Oreos or something), don't eat (a diet plan of some kind with before and after photos); eat nutritionally (what the hell does that mean), prepare a quick meal; prepare a nutritional quick meal, don't eat -- drink *Slim Fast*; blah, blah and more blah.

Jeez ladies, you're getting beat to death with this crap.

Have you ever asked yourself why?

'Cause the purveyors of the products are making some serious dinero off of you, that's why (Weight Watchers Inc. has sales of almost 2 billion with about 13% profit margin).

They're making the money because the Moguls, the medical Moguls, the clothing Moguls, the fitness Moguls, etc. have invented and continually reinvent *their* definition of what a "correct" weight should be. They, with their army of psychologists, statisticians, and other pseudo-scientists, have confused the hell out of everyone, completely understand the confusion and will do anything in their power to keep the confusion alive.

They won't allow you to know whether you're fat or skinny or, heaven forbid, "normal". .

Men don't pay much attention because the female/male rule and its associated lies imply that men are OK and women are not. To state it another way, women must conform to the prevailing standard of "attractiveness" that is in vogue to have value. Men just have to be around.

"It took a lot of beer to make this belly!"

Question: why is it that there are no women who are, to an absolute certainty, OK with their weight?

It has to do with definition.

Here's what I mean.

If you were to ask anyone: "What color is an apple?"

"Ripe? They may ask.

"Ripe."

"Red."

"What color red?"

Now we are getting into the nuts and bolts of definition.

If you did a little research on color, you would find the color of something depends on the frequency of the light wave emitted by an object as well as the ability of the receptors to analyze that particular frequency. In the case of folks, the receptors are the rods and cones in the eye and the ability of the brain to process and identify what the little buggers pick up. That's how we know color and everything else we see. It all depends on how well our eyes work in conjunction with the brain.

"Aha!" You may exclaim. "What you see as red may not be the same as what I see, yet we both use the same word."

With that simple question about an apple you have discovered the very essence of what the process of understanding or knowing is and it is immensely complicated. If no two people can actually see the same color red (there are a nearly infinite number of hues) how can they agree on something subtler, say "pretty".

The simple answer is that they can't.

How on earth do we communicate at all?

The simple answer is: not very well, but we do *seem* to go through a series of compromises.

Do you *see* what I'm saying?

If a couple want to paint the nursery in anticipation of a new arrival to the family, it is obvious that the female of the pair would never think of sending the male to go get some green paint. God knows what he would bring back! Conversely the male, assuming his knuckles don't drag on the ground and has half a brain, would never do such a thing. They will reach an understanding of what "green" is and the nursery will get painted and be ready for its precious occupant.

Compromise.

Not so much I'm right, you're wrong and let's meet in the middle kind of compromise, rather a mutual understanding between two people, <u>at that moment of time</u>, as to what "green" looks like.

Do they both agree that the color in question is actually "green"? Not at all. What they have agreed to is the abstraction of the color. Whatever shade of green our couple agreed upon has a very specific definition. It has a certain wavelength or a specific hexadecimal code for computer geeks, but people do not communicate in that fashion, so they abstract or remove enough qualities of the object in order to reach agreement. Thus people may agree that an apple is round, when it is not; is red when it is not; tastes sweet when it doesn't and so forth.

I don't know if you picked up on it yet, but I'm talking about language. We don't have much trouble with verbs, nouns, prepositions and those kinds of words. All the commotion is caused by adjectives. You know, descriptors: the *white* house, the *tall* man, the *ugly* ape – those kinds of words.

Nasty business those adjectives but they are absolutely necessary because they lend flavor to what we want to say and how we see the world.

One could describe a box and say:

"The box was 5.75 inches long by 3.5 inches wide and 2.0 inches deep. The wooden sides were carved. The lid was covered with pieces of nacre."

Or you could say:

"The box was a lovely piece. It seemed to be large enough to hold two decks of playing cards side by side. The box's wooden sides were carved with small geometric designs resembling Egyptian hieroglyphics and were quite charming but the lid was its most striking feature. It was delicately inlayed with a mosaic of shimmering slices of mother of pearl placed with care to reveal the figure of a dog sitting quietly as if waiting for its master's call."

Same box, different picture.

Life would be dull indeed without adjectives. Actually, life would be whatever life is, but we would describe it dully and, as that Danish guy, Hamlet, would say: "…ay, there's the rub."

Not only do we use words to describe the world as we see it to others, but we use words to describe the world as we see it to ourselves, and act accordingly. Thus what we perceive is our reality but it is not necessarily another person's reality.

Change the words and your reality changes.

An African-American used to be a black person, or if you go back a little further a Negro or nigger.

Different words, different image and a change in our reality.

OK, OK, big duh here. Everybody knows that, but most everybodies don't think about it that way and get themselves into a big mess because they act out their lives as if the words are reality.

That collection of grunts, wheezes, snorts and clicks that we call words have, as we all know, incredible power. Wars are started and ended through the use of words; people are classified, catalogued and often disparaged by words; communities govern or anarchy prevails with words, crimes are defined and penalties, even death penalties, are/are not carried out by the use of words; terror and security succeed with words; enough already – you get the idea.

Certain words mess with our heads and make us do weird things. The worst words are those that have vague definitions.

Beautiful leaps to mind.

Several people can agree with each other that a sunset may be beautiful, or a painting, or even a mathematical equation, but human physical configuration or looks…not so much agreement.

As we grow up, we are infused with a whole lexicon of words that are indefinable, absurdly abstract, possibly dangerous or at least expensive.

Many of those words are primarily directed at women by our society as a result of thousands of years believing that a woman's only worth is as an object of beauty.

Beautiful, cute, pretty, plain, plain Jane, fat, skinny, full-bodied, big boned, smooth, silky, vibrant, lustrous, creamy, perky, well rounded, youthful, bouncy and etc.

All descriptors of appearance, not substance.

Actually they are ad-speak words.

I don't know for sure, but I suspect that a conversation like this never takes place:

"Doesn't Carol's skin look creamy smooth today?" Veronica asked Betty.

"Oh yes, and her hair is so lustrous and bouncy."

Was that real or was it Memorex?

Neither, it would be a conversation invented by advertisers: ad-speak.

Since appearance is such an important part of satisfying the attractiveness part of the female/male rule and since what is "good" appearance is difficult to define, the advertising community (lackeys of the Feminine Industrial Complex) has gleefully jumped in and provided "definitions".

They have invented or rearranged words to tell you what "good" appearance is; words that are the mainstay of creating insecurity in order to sell their products.

Here's the way it works. They have a table (see below) called a "Madison Avenue Mogul Buzz Word Generator" with three columns and ten rows. Say they want to "define" a product; they pick three numbers at random and use the corresponding words.

	1	2	3
1	Bouncy	Vibrant	Youthful
2	Vibrant	Creamy	Vibrant
3	Lustrous	Lustrous	Smooth
4	Creamy	Luxurious	Silky
5	Perky	Perky	Sensual
6	Luxurious	Sensual	Perky
7	Smooth	Silky	Luxurious
8	Silky	Smooth	Lustrous
9	Youthful	Bouncy	Creamy
10	Sensual	Youthful	Bouncy

For instance 2,4,8 (vibrant, luxurious, lustrous) and then attach the part of the female body they for which they wish to promote their product.

Thus:

With daily use of Snot Cream, you too can have vibrant, luxurious and lustrous skin.

Or

With daily use of Snot Cream, you too can have vibrant, luxurious and lustrous hair.

Or

With daily use of Snot Cream, you too can have vibrant, luxurious and lustrous eyelashes.

They would probably use a better name than Snot Cream, but you get the idea. Combine the sentence with a picture and they have created yet another unattainable image.

I particularly like the phrase "clinically tested". What does that mean? What did they test? What were the results? What clinic? What did they test for? What, what, what?

At least it wasn't a garage.

Maybe it was.

Hmmmm.

Here are just a few words that are associated with ideas that no one can live up to: handsome, manly, virile, in-charge, the boss, decisive, muscular, powerful; or their counterparts: beautiful, feminine, sexy, lady-like, compassionate, queen of the manor, curvaceous, the fairer sex.

There are hundreds more that are pounded into our heads from birth.

Most people try to handle the barrage of crap handed out by advertisers with varying degrees of success but frequently fail. We are assaulted daily by professionals armed with the latest psychological weaponry and in spite of our best efforts some of the ad-speak words do sneak through and mess with our heads.

Fat!

Now there's a word for you. Fat is bad, bad to eat, bad to be. The word fat is so bad that it's often not used in "polite company". The word fat is so bad that a whole bunch of words are used to say the same thing but are selected to take the edge off.

"Honey, you're not fat, you're big boned. You know, full-bodied."

full-bodied – *adj.* Having richness and intensity of flavor. Said of wines.

See, call her fat but take the edge off with words that don't have anything to do with what you're talking about – ad-speak.

Doesn't quite do it, but close enough.

I like the word *corpulent*. Technically, in some dictionaries, corpulent and obese are synonyms, but I don't see it that way. I derive my meaning from the Spanish, *cuerpo,* or body. *Me gusta una mujer con cuerpo,* I like a woman with body, which implies some meat. No angularity. No bones sticking out. Cheeks instead of hollows. Give me a woman with some flesh anytime. Corpulence also implies, to me, strength, something regal and sexy for sure! You know Marilyn Monroe corpulent – 5'-5" and between 140 and 150 pounds, probably a size 12-14 dress – some *corpus* but firm.

Having said all of that, the reality is that regardless of external configuration, if the internal configuration is nonexistent or bland, the outward stuff matters not at all. That's why to me a person like Paris Hilton or Lindsay Lohan or many other "celebrities" are seriously unattractive. They have all the "right" accouterments – thin, fashionable, good body, etc. – but behave like dolts making them, in my mind, unattractive.

Back to fat.

Until recently, 500 years ago, plus or minus a couple of decades, corpulence was the size of choice for ladies and skinny was definitely out.

Fat in women made sense. In the olden days, old, olden days, being corpulent meant you could withstand hard times (famine, pestilence, plague) and care for the young.

Skinny? – Toast.

Some young girls were skinny but that deficiency was soon repaired.

"Ah Madonna. Look at you! You are skin and bones! *Mangia, mangia* hava some pasta!"

Everybody was pretty much OK with that.

All the fertility goddesses of old were fat; some seriously fat.

Enter the Industrial Revolution, mass marketing and Disney's Cinderella. Suddenly, particularly in the last several decades, corpulence is out and size 4 is in.

Rats!

Naturally, most women can't get into a size 4 so the manufacturers, now well accustomed to lying to anyone who will listen, make up new sizes. In fact, the design dimensions for a particular size varies from manufacturer to manufacturer or even within the same brand. Thus a size 10 may now be a size 4 or maybe a 12 – who knows? The Moguls just change the size numbers and invent new ones like petit long or some such dawdle and the ladies put up with it.

Amazing.

Cinderella looks anorexic. She probably is, hanging out near the fireplace and all. Ugly little broad! She probably has a bad attitude too. Skinny chicks are that way.

Sorry about the broad and chicks thing.

Anyhow, social pressure to keep the feminine rule alive and the incessant hammering of the Complex shamelessly hawking their goods, keeps women all fired up.

Even the coolest of women, and I know many; at some time decide they're fat. If you are 5'6 and weigh 250 pounds, you're obese and you're going to die. If you're the same height and weigh 150 pounds, not fat.

Don't look at me; I consulted the weight tables.

Be careful here because the original weight tables were established by an insurance company based on mortality rates not health and the weight loss and medical Moguls keep changing the numbers.

Regardless, for some mysterious reason the lady decides she's fat. Maybe her pants are too snug, or maybe she feels more comfortable in a larger dress size, or maybe her pal, Ethel, just lost five pounds and she's envious, or maybe she was shopping and wanted to buy a certain outfit and couldn't find it in her size, whatever. She's decided she's fat and no amount of persuasion can convince her otherwise.

Don't try.

The weirdness begins.

First she'll look for confirmation and ask if you think she's fat.

I have no idea if women ask other women if they're fat and if they did I can't imagine what the conversation would be like. I am certain, however, that honesty, compassion and friendliness would not be the hallmark of that conversation.

Confirmation seems to be the male's responsibility.

Why? I have no clue.

A little advice for the males here. Pay attention! You can see the question coming and you can either head off the confrontation at the pass or bear the consequences. There are signs, all different depending on the lady, but there are signs never the less. Daily, and I mean DAILY, look at your woman with something other than your crotch. I know she's fine, but that's not even close to the point. Has there been a little shift in proportionality? A little bulge here, a little sag there? Looser clothes? Changes in menu? A lot of salads? Get a clue man! Remember, you want peace, *Monday Night Football* and a little nooky now and then.

Or you may not care and like her fat and maybe she doesn't care either.

Assuming she does, she will eventually ask the dreaded question but, if you've been paying attention, you will be prepared with an appropriate response that will be supportive of her vaguely defined quest. If you're really good, you'll get that nooky.

Fatness has been established and dieting begins.

Contrary to all logic and medical science, women set a deadline for their reconfiguration.

"I need to lose ten pounds by next month so I can get into that dress for the party!"

That whole thought process is weird.

Let's reword.

"I saw this dress and it's (insert word: gorgeous, sexy, elegant, etc.; numbers 6,10,3 on the weight loss Moguls Buzz Phrase Generator). I need to get it because it would really make me look (insert one or all of the words previously listed) for the party next month..."

Somebody snuck into her head and created an image that she wants to fulfill. She wants to look like something that she *thinks* she is not.

Weird.

"Why'd she do that?"

Let's suppose, for purposes of discussion, that you are a successful, professional, forty one year old lady, about 5'7" and weigh about 140 pounds. Sounds pretty nice to me.

One day you notice that one of your business suits seems to be a little snug.

Rush to the scales.

"My God! 152 pounds!"

You strip down and examine yourself in the mirror.

"What happened to my waist? My boobs are sagging much more than I had noticed. Shit! I'm getting fat!"

It makes no difference to you whatsoever that there is a healthy weight variance of plus or minus 20 pounds for any person of a particular height.

Vows are made. No more martinis after work and those nachos have to go! Need to go to the gym regularly.

All good things.

Two weeks go by, and there's no significant change.

You weigh 150 pounds. Some progress, but you still have ten pounds to go.

Right about here is where some ladies go nuts.

"Lose ten pounds in one week with no effort!"

(Ten pounds seems to be some kind of magical number in ad-speak. Why not eight and a half or eleven?)

It makes absolutely no difference that no one else has noticed or even remotely cares. Your man still lusts after you, your business associates still value your opinion (particularly if you don't wear makeup) and you haven't heard any catty remarks from your friends.

Ad-speak starts to make sense. Diet plan commercials, once ignored, are now the focus of your attention. You may even buy a book or two.

You start to get a little bitchy. No wonder, you have disrupted your routine, your eating habits, maybe even your sex life.

You notice, for reasons of comparison, all of your lady friends' weight and begin to converse with them on the subject.

Sympathy, consolation, support (maybe) and advice – lots of advice – is received and given.

Days go by and still no significant change.

By now, all logic is gone and you begin a cycle of weight gain, weight loss and the Complex is dancing with glee while they rake in your hard-earned money spent on programs that don't work.

Just for information purposes, the three major weight-loss companies rake in about four billion dollars a year – a lot of dough.

Here are some facts:

Fact: you are forty, pushing fifty; your body is going to change and gravity works.

Fact: a bunch of people love you, regardless.

Fact: your business associates could care less.

Fact: to maintain weight as you get older; eat less.

Etc., Etc.

So back to my original question: Why'd she to that?

I don't know.

I can only suppose that she succumbed to a blind belief that somehow she is inadequate and that belief has gained control of her wisdom and no matter how much arguing or cajoling anyone may do, even the most rational of ladies seem to reject the notion that one's height and weight are pretty much predisposed by genetics.

By the way, being on the high side or even ten or twenty pounds over any weight table's definition of proper weight for your height is meaningless if you are fit and follow an exercise regimen. Athletes have high body mass indices and are off the scale of weight tables yet are healthy.

Fat doesn't necessarily mean unhealthy.

Do we all get a little overweight from time to time?

You betcha.

Do we all have to stop shoveling in food occasionally?

Same answer, but to diet to try and look like some imaginary ethereal vision probably created and communicated by ad-speak – weird.

Another thing, when did we attach a moral value to food?

Food is completely neutral. Chocolate cake is chocolate cake, no more, no less.

If you should decide to have piece of chocolate cake at home or while dinning out, you are having a piece of cake, you are not indulging. Having six slices at one time is a little weird and will probably make you puke or get diarrhea but the cake is just the cake.

Salads are not "good", they are salads. Eating nothing but salads will probably get the same results as too much cake but the salad is just a salad.

Eating "healthy", which is supposed to be good, depends entirely on the individual and whatever particular fad is in vogue at the time. If you are eating "unhealthy" your body will let you know if you just listen. If you are lethargic, have trouble sleeping, are gaining weight, losing weight, bad skin, constipated, lots of colds and other things that make you feel a little out of kilter, you are probably eating poorly for your body. Make a list of what you eat, how much and figure it out.

Not hard.

On a personal note, my wife went through a bad weight issue some time ago. I didn't say a word even though she had passed 200 pounds. I knew that she knew and was struggling to comprehend her problem.

Eventually, she confessed that she was fat.

I didn't say anything. I cooed and consoled and together we set out on a plan. We cut out almost all fat. She ate a lot of salads and vegetables (she doesn't care much for fruit). I took over the bulk of the cooking. It was fun. I discovered all kinds of recipes that are good and pretty much fat free – we still eat that way. She snacked on carrot sticks and *Slim Fast*.

To complete the picture I hired a personal trainer as a surprise Christmas gift. He was a seriously handsome young man which I'm sure didn't hurt. He came to the house and spent a month showing her an exercise routine. For two years she worked her butt off on her own. She hated it, but she did it and I will always admire her.

Two years and the loss of 50+ pounds later, peace reigns in the kingdom.

Change in lifestyle? Not really. The carrot sticks, *Slim Fast* and most salads are gone as well as the fat and large portions. Infrequent meals to restaurants are now guiltless delicious adventures instead of what we used to believe were a requirement due to schedules or laziness.

I truly believe that she was successful because she was <u>not</u> trying to look like something else; she succeeded because she reached the configuration that is genetically normal for her and I'm convinced that her brain kicked in and said "OK we're fine now" and conscious dieting is no longer required.

She was "dressing" from the inside.

As with my wife, most women handle their obsession with weight pretty well, i.e.: a minimum amount of weirdness.

Unfortunately some women are genetically predisposed to be fat and that's a serious problem that requires medical attention, not some charlatan on television.

Some other ladies, and fortunately there only a few, get WEIRD. For those unfortunate ladies, the obsession to look like or be someone who they are not, leads to anorexia or bulimia; a perfect example of ad-speak and image creation by the Complex gone to extreme.

"It's not my fault!" Cries the Mogul.

Yeah right. Maybe if you hadn't created that impossible, unobtainable image and then written lies about ineffectual plans to try and reach that image…

Hell, this discussion is pointless. Anyhow, Mr. or Ms. Mogul I spit on you.

Those jerks have become so adroit at their lies that they now pander this stuff as news and ladies lap it up.

"Mary Kay Olsen… (maybe it's the other one, I don't know)…was admitted to (inset name) clinic due a severe eating disorder."

Or

"The beautiful star of (some stupid show, song or whatever) was seen about town and she looks a little largish. Please (insert name), don't tell us you are binging."

There are all kinds of weirdness going on here.

That someone has the *cojones* to even print that stuff is weird.

What do those people do when they get up in the morning?

"I think I'll go down to the beach and see if I can get some pictures of so-and-so's cellulite.

Now there's a rewarding career.

"What did you do at work today, Daddy?"

"I went to the beach and shot pictures of middle-aged women's butts."

Parent day at school must be really swell for that family!

Pictures go to the publisher and they have meetings about how much crap they can invent without getting sued, where to place the story and which ads to precede and follow the story.

The cover is discussed – usually a provocative photo of some star, supermodel or celebrity.

"I love the pose, but it needs more airbrushing."

I kid you not, I saw Kelly Ripa on the cover of some magazine with enormous boobs. What's up with that? She's a lovely lady, a good comic and probably a nice person. Big boobs? No. Why did the editors feel compelled to mess with her body?

Weird.

Tangential issue here. What is the fascination with celebrities?

Actors and most celebrities play roles that someone has created for them and many are fascinating in those roles. Their personal lives? Hardly.

Actors are clowns and their job is to entertain us. They appear to have moderate intelligence, questionable common sense and a flair for the dramatic (they're actors –duh). A few actors are highly paid, most are starving.

Almost nothing that you read about them is true.

"But they are so glamorous!"

That's the nature of their trade. Nobody gets parts by sitting around their apartment. If you want to command a multi-million dollar fee for your services, you'd better be glamorous. They have to see and be seen. They have to create a buzz so that producers and casting people believe that the public will spend money to see them perform.

Virtually nothing about their public persona is real. That's why they are called actors.

So what's the fascination?

Weird.

One of the side effects of this entire camera snooping and lies is that these mags get sued a lot and lose. The other is that they don't seem to give the objects of their snooping much rest or privacy.

Here's a question for some lawyers:

Let's suppose that an actor, say Angelina Jolie, that doesn't want to get pestered. Why can't she become a corporation with her face as the corporation's trademark? Then anyone who uses her face without her permission is violating trademark laws. Kellogg's Tony the Tiger is a trademark, why can't Ms. Jolie be one?

I have no idea if that is possible or not, but the entertainment value of trying to make it so would be enormous.

Anyhow, back to the magazine.

The rag with the butt pictures and story hits the newsstand and sells a zillion copies, mostly to ladies. Countless women look in the mirror and discover that they too have cellulite (it's a genetic thing – get over it, you're still hot).

Bunches and bunches of creams, lotions, exercise plans are sold. Spas spring up that will shoot you with electric prods or laser beams to banish the offending bumps. Note that a few months ago you either didn't notice or didn't care that you had bumps and the guy you're boinking for sure doesn't care.

Manufacturers and spa owners are elated. They spend more money on advertising. Ad agencies are in full swing and invent words like "smoothing lotion" and "tightening therapy". The magazines rake in more advertising dollars and send the slug (can't call him a pig – it's an honor thing) of a photographer out to dig up or invent something new.

All is well in the Feminine Industrial Complex fueled by female dollars and abetting casual sexism.

Why are you ladies compelled to support this abominable offence on common decency?

Why do you buy trash that assaults you and hammers away at your *imagined* inadequacies?

That's right, IMAGINED. Imagined, imagined, imagined, imagined.

Casual sexism at work.

Is the madness going to change?

It can change if you want it to.

Instead of wasting your energy attacking us men for our apparent lack of sensitivity, why not use the power you have and snuff out the madness. What do you think would happen if all the women stopped buying those magazines say, *Cosmopolitan* or *US* or *The National Enquirer*, or whatever for six months?

You have the power to demand that you be treated with respect and it costs you nothing!

It isn't even an inconvenience.

Make the bastards and bitches sweat. Tell them, with power of <u>not</u> opening your purse that you don't need to know what turns him on and don't care. Tell them that you want to know how you can save us all from ultimate chaos with the power of your optimism, the skill of your mind and the force of your energy!

Chaos is coming sports fans, and only women can avert it.

Is the madness going to change?

Apparently not.

Do you care?

Apparently not.

Then I guess all I can say is:

Screw you! And I don't want to hear about your weight bullshit!

Ladies and gentlemen, as a nation we all eat too much.

Knock it off!

Further, I don't want to hear any more whining about how men objectify you. You are doing it to yourselves by accepting the fallacy of the words as if they were real. There is no real definition for beautiful, or sexy, or any other of those stupid words – there is only you!

Men are not the enemy. You have met the enemy and it is you!

You have struggled and attained some measure of legal and social equality don't piss it away by obsessing about your weight as if skinny is beautiful. And, just like I say to the men, don't think with your crotch.

You want to obsess over something? Obsess over poverty, hunger, your children, the business you are buildings, the law's delay, the insolence of office or the pangs of despised love.

Obsessing about your weight or some ethereal concept of beauty?

It's embarrassing!

It's embarrassing because, except for health reasons, the exercise is a pointless attempt to be attractive as demanded by the Complex's concept of femininity that demands that you be available to breed. You refuse to acknowledge that the definition of attractiveness varies with time and place, the information surrounding it is often contradictory and the rule itself comes from ancient myths modified by time and opportunity, embellished by lies perpetrated by people with special interests and a dash of nonsense thrown in for entertainment value.

The only thing important about your weight is your health.

Period!

Do not buy into the argument that proposes that there is some predisposed heredity thing going on that demands that women be "attractive".

Nope. I've got to discount that because different cultures of our species have different views on physical configuration and all of us seem to survive and multiply fairly well.

Also that concept presumes that women are trapped by their genetic makeup to forever quest to become the "ideal" woman and men must be macho and control everything.

Can't buy that. No individual human is trapped by anything. We all have physical and psychological plusses and minuses that challenge us. Some of us do better than others, but none of us are trapped. Besides, if we are genetically predisposed to do something then all of us would do the same thing – which we don't.

Some statistician or geneticist will probably come up with some argument to the contrary based on "exhaustive" research but they can't prove anything, they can only cite probabilities.

Probabilities don't mean squat to *you* the individual!

One thing is sure; the Moguls are getting rich by bilking women, and by extension the whole society. Billions of dollars and tons of scarce resources and thousands of animals are tortured for the sole purpose of assaulting women with the idea that they have flaws that can only be "solved" if their products are purchased or their "life style" adhered to.

Buying into that is a little diminishing, don't you think?

Three

You Are What You Look Like – Really?

Let's talk about makeup, one of the most powerful perpetrators of casual sexism.

There is nothing wrong with applying makeup. People, men and women, have been using it for centuries and its use is not going to disappear any time soon. It is so ingrained in our culture that there is hardly a woman alive that feels comfortable without just a little makeup.

The purpose of makeup is to create an illusion. What the illusion should be is open for discussion but the standards are usually set by the Moguls of the Feminine Industrial Complex like Maybelline, Cover Girl, etc. because they supply the products and instruct on its application.

It's big business and because it's big business they have to keep sales up so they will invent new products and develop new looks. Smokey eyes, purple lipstick or green nail polish for instance.

Makeup users, mostly women, will vary the style and amount of makeup depending on the occasion and illusion they wish to create. All good except it's not clear who decides what the illusion should be. Is it the user or the manufacturer, celebrity, talk-show person, your mother...who?

What about the amount? Should it be just a little blush and lipstick or is eye shadow, eye liner and/or mascara required?

Sometimes the user might run out of stuff or has let the bottle open and it's dried out.

Are substitutions allowed? If so, what?

It's a little confusing and maybe even unsettling.

Confusion and apprehension aside, I don't think anyone would suggest that one should go out and face the ogres of industry or go to a cool party without a reasonably good appearance. Everyone has to shit, shower, shave and brush their teeth before venturing out of doors. Having a whole populace running around with hair sticking up and dragon breath would be unseemly to say the least, but there's preparation and then there's PREPARATION.

Many women believe that they must PREPARE.

Why?

A woman will tell you that she wants to look nice, professional, neat, sharp, sexy, presentable or whatever when she leaves her abode and to achieve that effect takes some effort.

Admirable, assuming that if one looks the part, one is the part.

If you look "nice", are you nice? If you look "professional", are you professional?

I'm not so sure, but I know the entire world thinks so.

Let me say that again:

THE ENTIRE WORLD THINKS SO.

That's a lot of pressure and for you ladies it's unfair, unreasonable and downright nasty.

Who decides what the "look" should be and why?

I'd like to find that son or daughter of a wayward dog and thrash him/her.

Kapooy! Whack! Right in the kisser.

Actually, I didn't have to look too hard. One of the bad guys is Disney.

"Disney? Not possible!"

Yup, 'cause he produced *Cinderella.*

Everyone knows the story of Cinderella and knows that it's a fairy tale, a myth or some such thing. You know that because if the story had any spark of reality she would have grown up got pregnant and run off with some farm boy or whomever. Or if the story took place now, she would have murdered her stepmother and her stepsisters in their beds and claimed domestic abuse, insanity or that she was PMSing. Of course Cinderella is a fairy tale and reality has no place in those kinds of stories.

Anyhow, Cinderella was dealt a bad hand and she was coping as well as she could. Apparently she was a comely lass, at least relative to her relatives. Eventually, as we all know, she got the help of some old woman with magical powers, some rats and other farm animals, snuck into the ball, charmed the prince and eventually, after some searching on his part for dramatic effect, he placed the shoe on her foot and she married the handsome prince and lived happily ever after.

An innocuous story?

Not so. Insidious is a more accurate term.

in·sid·i·ous *adj.* Intended to entrap; wily; treacherous…

Here's the problem. The basic premise is that Cinderella, although by all accounts was pretty, was invisible until she put on the beautiful dress, got jeweled up, had her hair done and slipped on those perfect slippers. She went to the ball and no one recognized her. She wasn't Cinderella anymore; she was a Princess because *she looked the part.* Back at the fireplace, she couldn't be a Princess because *she didn't look the part.* As a matter of fact, the stepmother, stepsisters and even the twit of a Prince didn't recognize her as the Princess of the ball. All they saw was the char girl. Naturally, no coiffure, no jewels, no dress – how could she be a Princess? Even after His Majesty the Twit put the slipper on there was some waffling on his part.

That's the whole message to the story: you are not you, you are what you look like and if you want to look like something, you have to have magic to do it.

Herbal Essence anyone?

The flip side of the story is that all the male characters are vacuous. The female characters are evil or wonderfully kind or something in between thus establishing the multidimensionality of females and the flatness of the males. Besides, she went after him not the other way around and the implication is that to have status a girl must marry a prince regardless of his ineffectuality.

Women are nothing without a charming prince.

Not a good message.

Not to mention the fact that there are no charming princes and never have been. Kind of screws up your expectations, don't you think?

You may say that this little cartoon movie can't possibly have an effect on women's behavior.

Maybe so but the problem is that this story, in a variety of versions but with the same theme, has been around for centuries. The first known written version is found in a collection of stories compiled and written in 860 by a fellow named Tuan Ch'ing-Shih. His Cinderella was called Yen-Shen and he got the story from folklore. Many authors in many countries like Serbia, Russia, Ireland, England, Demark, and Kashmir to name a few, wrote their own version of the story. In 1950, Disney just took Perrault's 1697 version and made it the standard the whole world accepts.

Been around a long time and read or told to millions of little girls for over 1,000 years. You bet your bippy it has had an effect. As we speak, that story in all its glory is probably being absorbed by, I don't know, one hundred little girls. That's twenty-four hundred a day, about 900,000 a year, etc.

There have been bunches of novels and stories made from this theme, e.g.: *Don't tell Mom the Baby Sitter's Dead* and *Working Girl*.

Both use the premise that smart young women are unrecognized (Cinderella) and by a quirk of fate (Fairy God Mother) change their appearance and assume roles in the business world (go to the ball). Circumstances get out of control (midnight), but a handsome prince forgives all or some such dawdle.

The latest assault on what little girls think they should look like is Disney's makeover of Merida, the heroine of the movie *Brave*. In the original version by Pixar, Merida had an ordinary figure, frizzy hair and no makeup, Disney made her over with an hourglass figure, flowing locks, and a bit of a plunging neckline which proves once again that you can't be a princess unless you look the part – at least from Disney's point of view.

Zillions of little girls are taught that who they are is less important than what they look like and the result is a culture that values women for their appearance and pays little or no attention to her character, intelligence or the power of her being.

Do not assume that men are not under similar pressures. External beauty is not as much of an issue for men but strength, height and muscularity are big issues for men, particularly when they are younger. Sensitivity, compassion and empathy are not traits high on the list of importance. Then, of course, there is money and power or at least the appearance of them. Gotta be the prince, remember?

After all, the lovely Cinderella went after the prince, not the butcher, the baker or the candlestick maker.

Big lie. Popular lie.

If you have a big popular lie that is accepted by almost everyone, you can count on someone making a buck off of that popularity. Not by selling the story, that's small potatoes, but by cashing in on the theme: you gotta look the part or you're invisible!

Enter the Feminine Industrial Complex.

When this Industrial Complex came into being is not clear but today their combined gross revenues are enormous. Their purpose is to make money by convincing women that their products will make them beautiful and members of the Complex are the ones that define what beautiful is or is not. They do their convincing through the use of advertising.

There are essentially two types of advertising. One imparts information and the other projects an image. Sometimes they blend together. The image type implies that you are not as valuable as you could be and if you use their product, your value will increase. Thus, by definition, this kind of advertising creates insecurity.

Clothes, shoes, hair products, jewelry, lipstick, makeup and other stuff are pimped by the Feminine Industrial Complex and they pay the owners of thousands of men and women's magazines, talk shows and even the news to display their wares. The magazines, shows or whatever then pray on the fears and insecurities of countless people, mostly women. Fears and insecurities that are kept alive by the very specialized media that claims to help. An article here, ten advertisements there, all designed to make you spend money on crap you don't really need.

Men are not immune but women are the primary target.

For instance, when I was a lad, there were advertisements on the back of comic books extolling the virtues of a strong body. A young boy tries to talk to a girl at the beach and a bully comes along and kicks sand in his face. "Don't let this happen to you." The ad screamed. "Buy the Charles Atlas body building equipment." Now we talk about abs and pecs and other male parts and the message is the same: you are less of a man if you don't look like this! Don't forget your Viagra or free-testosterone pills.

Advertising may be described as the science of arresting intelligence long enough to get money from it.

-- Stephen Leacock

That Tuan Ch'ing-Shih dude sure did start something.

Little girls aren't stupid. They can see the connection all around them. This dress means this, that hairstyle means that and so on. The whole myth of image is fostered by their mothers, aunts, older sisters or any other female authority figure.

Mom: works hard, a little frazzled, loving but not powerful – clothes from Target.

Professional woman, movie star, news anchor or talk show host: works hard, organized, powerful – clothes from Saks.

"My, you're such a pretty little girl!"

Every woman is susceptible to the onslaught and it works to the tune of billions of dollars a year.

Does it have to?

It's up to you.

The next time you buy a magazine, look at an ad, watch TV or whatever, process the information in terms of need and necessity. Ask yourselves this: "Am I really nasty looking? Do I need to look like the spokesperson or model? Does the man or woman I'm with really care?" If your answer is yes, you might be in trouble. If your answer is no, the worst that will happen is that you save a little money, the best will be that the morning ritual will be faster, less stressful and will add to your confidence. You will be in control and you will go out and face the world on your own terms.

Cinderella was still Cinderella regardless of what she looked like.

Unfortunately, the preparation required covers a lot of territory. Not only are women lied to about what their face and hair should or must be like, but their attire, bodies and general demeanor are also targets of the Complex's insatiable lust after her money. Men are not immune to the assault but not to the same degree.

Let's start at the top of the head – hair.

There are few universal truths in this life, but one of them is that if a lady has curly hair, at some time she wants straight hair. The converse to that truism is also valid and a whole bunch of variations on the same theme.

If your hair is your "crowning glory" and you want it, and by extension you, to be attractive and I presume that you want to attract men.

Why bother? Men don't much care as long as it's clean.

Of course there is the possibility that you want to attract women, in which case…???

Nobody wants to look like dudu, therefore, a certain amount of maintenance is required and correctly so, but ladies, complete reconstruction?

By now you know what has happened.

Cinderella.

A clever advertiser portrays a young woman with shimmering (their word, not mine) hair, which she tosses around and it falls neatly into place.

A vision sneaks into your head.

You don't care or are ignorant of the fact that there is an army of hairstylists poised to be sure that the right affect is portrayed; that the shimmering comes from the cameraperson's lights; that filters are used on the lens; that the fifteen second spot required hundreds of takes and that the actress/model doesn't wear her hair in that fashion. Don't forget CGI.

The Witches of Weird are loose and you are off. New color, new perm, new cut and guess what happens:

Your guy may or may not notice!

Bummer!

Those of you in the hairstyling business know what I'm talking about here. I bet you can't count the number of times that some lady has come into your shop and requested a new do with little or no backup data. No picture, no example, no nothing, just a vague idea of what she wants. She may even be unclear as to the color.

You try your best even though you may know that the style she requests really doesn't suit her face and possibly her hair doesn't grow the way she wants it shaped. In the end, of course, it's your fault that the thing didn't turn out right and you may lose a customer.

Do they teach mind reading in hairstylist school?

Smart women dabble in this kind of activity from time to time and its fun. It's fun because you know who you are and you don't obsess. You know with a reasonable degree of certainty that your man is with you because you are you. You also know that if he's with you because of your appearance alone, his visit will be short – hopefully because you will kick his sorry ass out into the street.

We can move down the head and repeat the same story.

What's with luxurious lashes?

For what it's worth, I invited about twenty guys over and conducted a survey. It took a while and some beer to get past the tits and ass thing but they eventually settled down.

I asked their opinions on about hair, nails, noses, makeup in general, weight and all kinds of stuff. Not very scientific but the general consensus was that we men will never figure out how you decide how you should look and apparently, based on my "exhaustive" survey, men know that a woman is beautiful if he loves her and she loves him back.

Let me say that again.

To a man, a woman is beautiful if he loves her and she loves him back. Configuration is immaterial.

Period.

Bruno Mars says it in his song "Just the Way You Are".

> When I see your face
> There's not a thing that I would change
> 'Cause you're amazing
> Just the way you are

Interestingly enough, if you love yourself you will also be amazing just the way you are. No need to hide behind a mask. Love yourself, look in the mirror and guess what: you are seriously hot!

While the survey was being conducted, a thought kept running through my head: what if all women stopped concentrating on the futile attempt to become something they are not and minimally enhance who they are?

What would happen?

For one thing, there might be less ridiculing. Remember what I discovered: you are beautiful solely because you are loved and you return that affection. A little fat? A largish nose? So-so hair? He doesn't care, you shouldn't care and if someone else cares you need to question their motives.

If the effort and expense were toned down a bit, a couple of things might happen.

Temporary economic collapse for one thing. All the zillions of products fostered by the Cinderella myth would not be sold but you would be free. Free to be yourself and glory in whom you are.

The countless dollars and time now wasted to try to appear to be something you are not would be available to nurture who you are.

Someone once said that a person should dress from the inside out.

Maybe that also applies to eyeliner, foundation, mascara, lipstick, etc.

Think about it.

Anyhow, the incredible power of your mind and purse could be free of nonsense, and would be available to conquer poverty, disease and countless other social ills that we men can't seem to address much less solve!

To dream the impossible dream…

Oh well, ain't gonna happen.

Kind of sad actually.

There you have it. There seems to be a rule that states that women must be feminine and men must be masculine. No one is absolutely sure what that means but it doesn't matter since most of us accept a statement like that without truly understanding and act accordingly. For women, it is presumed that part of being feminine is to PREPARE your face, hair and other parts of your body to be "attractive".

There are a couple of flaws with this theory.

First, the amount and style of PREPARATION is not clear. It changes with time and location. What was proper and desirable in the 1990s is not the same as now and the standards are set by the manufacturers, not by the individual. What is proper and desirable at age 25 is not the same as age 60. What is proper and desirable in India is not the same as in Russia or China or the U.S.

Second, you may convince yourself that PREPARATION makes you feel better but you may actually be hiding who you are and as a result you may attract men or women that don't suit you and end up in a failed relationship.

Not good.

So you see, women are assaulted, almost from birth, with idealizations that are impossible to achieve and there seems to be a firm belief that with the proper PREPARATION one can achieve that ideal. I don't think anyone will argue that women spend a great deal of time, energy and money to PREPARE. The results of that effort are often pleasing and sometimes spectacular, but the person is still the person regardless.

From a historical perspective, Women have been PREPARING for centuries because it was essential that a woman snag a provider to survive. That requirement has slowly disappeared but the process lingers on for no apparent reason and as a result the effort is ridiculed by comedians and men in general.

There is, however, another possibility.

The 20th century brought about tremendous changes affecting a woman's status in society. Women became people instead of objects. They acquired some measure of legal and economic equality and the requirement that a woman needs a provider to survive essentially disappeared. PREPARATION however continued.

Why?

Let me throw something out for you to think about.

Could it have been that a woman's quest to PREPARE herself to face a hostile world was an expression of eternal optimism? An optimism that said, for example, today I have to be powerful so I will comb my hair this way, wear this makeup with these colors and charge the barricades. I know I am powerful and I'm going to make sure my outward appearance demonstrates that fact. Many may not agree, but by God I'm going to give it my best shot!

The same applied for her attempt to be nice, professional, neat, sharp, sexy, or whatever.

Her continual optimistic quest permeated the entire society and gave us all hope that, in spite of everything, we will succeed.

The glory of her efforts buoyed us all and spurred us to redouble our struggles to make life better, a little at a time.

Optimists do, pessimist sit home and sulk.

Lest you think that what I have suggested is bullshit, I can remember when there were no women in the workforce except in menial positions.

Those were drab places to be. Drab in design, drab in style, drab in creativity.

Women started to appear.

A flower here, a dash of color there, a little light and the workplace became transformed.

An enormous portion of how workplaces function today from design to safety to courtesy is a direct result of women transferring her optimistic preparations from her person to the factories, offices and stores.

Go to a Lowe's store. Lowe's target consumers are women. The store is clean, well lit, the floors are polished and the décor is coordinated. Home Depot caters to the contractors. The products are the same but the difference is obvious.

Workplaces are hugely better today almost exclusively because of the presence of women.

Now we are in the 21st century and we still cling to the thousands of years of false traditions that dictate what the outward appearance should be and ignore the fact that the optimism comes from within. What you look like may be nice but that impression fades very quickly and eventually you must demonstrate that you are, in fact, powerful – looks be damned.

This is a dilemma faced only by women.

This dilemma is most evident in the work environment. If you are going out to a party, a club or some other social function, PREPARATION makes sense, but for work, I'm not so sure.

I am definitely not sure in the 21st century.

Thousands of women before you have fought long and hard to assure that you have reasonably equal opportunities. They did not fight for you to be able to look good. Particularly if someone else defines what good is and worse if that someone wants your money as well.

Your mother? Well, you're on your own on that one.

Consider for a moment about what would happen if you went to work with no makeup at all – none.

You may think that people are looking at you strangely, but that's what you think, not necessarily what they think. Soon, you will adjust and find that all of the difficulties, challenges and successes will be identical.

You are chairing a meeting and making assignments. Do you honestly think that your instructions will be carried out more effectively because you are wearing makeup?

I think not.

Dump the foundation, blush, eyeliner, mascara, lipstick, etc., etc. and the high heels and bulky purse as well.

Try it.

Show your innate optimism by who you are; take off the mask and just be neat.

Save a bunch of time.

The disdain you perceive from your male coworkers or superiors will be the same but now you don't have to hide. I guarantee that your self-confidence will soar. You will be you and if they don't like it, you can sue them or tell them to fuck-off and die – not with that language, of course.

Party time? That's another story.

Remember that Revlon or Cover Girl or some other manufacturer are the only ones insisting that you must look a certain way to be valuable and they have been very effective at spreading that lie.

You are valuable because you have the training, the expertise and most of all, you are you.

I know, I know, you've read the surveys and probably experienced it yourself but just because there is the *impression* that women that look a certain way get most of the breaks doesn't mean that it has to continue.

Demand that it stop but be sure you're impression is accurate.

There is no law of nature that says that a pretty woman is, by definition, dumb.

There is absolutely no law of commerce that says that a "beautiful" woman is a better business person.

Currently we are in a bit of a complacent mode because we have forgotten how truly bad it used to be, but new challenges are just a few years away and brave women who laugh at the lies will buoy us with their optimism and we will overcome.

Therefore, I suggest that the process might be dumb but the reason is not. I also suggest that without the powerful presence of women in all facets of society, the world will be a drabber, sadder and a more dangerous place.

Men might take a lesson or two in this regard. A little preparation might go a long way. We all know you are a manly man, but a slob? We might consider trashing that ten-year old shirt and baggy shorts with a stain in the side…

Also, we men may like to think that a woman's PREPARATIONS are silly but we do the same thing. We cut our hair a certain way, we dress a certain way, we present ourselves in a certain way in order to create some image that we think will gain us acceptance. The difference is only a matter of degree but the process is the same.

So the next time you, mister manly man, catch yourself thinking that what a woman does is stupid – look in the mirror!

Oh shit! Where'd that nose hair come from?

Just a thought.

Be nice though if the Complex didn't sleaze up her efforts by continually being sexist and putting her down.

Be nice though if we remember who we are and get ready instead of PREPARING.

Be nice though if we remember that lies abound and not one single one of those lies has your interests at heart; their objective is to keep you subservient and steal your money.

Here's a little quiz: Does a person's perception of your intelligence, strength of character or general acumen increase or decrease in relation to your makeup application?

Four

Clothes, Clothes Everywhere and Not a Dress that Fits

Apparently, in most people's minds, one of the key elements of femininity is appearance. I'm not talking about physical configuration; I'm talking about external adornment. You know hair, makeup and clothes.

All of these things are used to create an illusion; an illusion to others as well as to yourself.

There is nothing inherently wrong with that except that the illusion is defined and created by someone other than the individual – the fashion industry part of the Feminine Industrial Complex.

There is a huge difference between clothes and fashion. Fashion is intended to make a statement, emphasize the most attractive features of the wearer (attractive depends on time and place) and distinguish the wearer from everyone else. Clothes protect you from the elements and help keep your skin clean.

Women invented fashion.

That should be no big surprise and it should be no big surprise that men took over and take credit.

No one knows how or when fashion instead of just clothes burst on the scene, so here's my take.

Back in the day, when we were prehistoric, folks were mostly naked. Yeah, they wore clothes some of the time, but they were mostly utilitarian things. You know protection from the elements.

Life marched on and except for animal attacks and an occasional marauding neighbor, the little group was happy.

There were a couple of problems however. Women got pregnant. Nobody knew how or why, but pregnant they got. The other problem was that the males, due primarily to their risky behavior, died a lot more frequently and there was always a surplus of women.

The pregnancy problem was a bummer because the female was not as available during pregnancy time to hunt and gather to supply food for the clan and she had to rely on one or more providers to keep her and her offspring afloat.

The surplus of females was also a problem because if a pregnant lady didn't have a provider during pregnancy and several years after, she would likely die.

Not good.

Obviously the women had to develop better techniques for attracting the men folk (or women folk – lesbians weren't invented yesterday you know).

An eland hide with some markings to add panache seemed to be the ticket.

Some of the ladies weren't pregnant but got dolled up anyway and invented the "oldest profession" to stay alive.

Suddenly there was competition and women started weaving cloth, stringing beads, sewing feathers and wearing clothes to keep their man at home. Naturally, women decided that their man should also wear clothes that she made so she could essentially put her mark on him.

The first fashion designers.

For the next several thousand years, clothes became more elaborate and complicated. Sewing became an absolute requirement for women and they probably invented the different materials, spinning wheels, looms, needles, threads, etc. Men, except for tailors, wouldn't do it, probably because they were inept and mostly they didn't care. As a matter of fact, men and women used to wear pretty much the same clothes; you know togas and skirts. The only significant difference is that men often wore an undergarment of some kind to keep their junk from swaying in the breeze.

Until the Industrial Revolution was in full swing, women made the vast majority of clothes in their homes. Most of that stuff was primarily utilitarian. An ordinary woman was lucky to have a decent

"Sunday-go-to-Meeting dress" and something of the same for their men and children. Otherwise, pretty plain and the emphasis was modesty for the women and decorum for the men.

Not much fashion innovation except for the rich and they pretty much went nuts. Rich women showed as much of their bodies as possible, primarily their bosoms, and men's fashions fluctuated between bizarre to… well, the weird. You know, Francis Drake and his crowd. See, the idea that a woman wanted her provider to look the part and be the most glorious "cock of the walk" idea hadn't disappeared and women dressed their men according to what women thought was cool.

Along comes the rise of the middle class. Now some folks had some bucks and what better way to spend it than emulating the rich. Not particularly noble, but there you have it: houses, horses, carriages and clothes – lots of clothes.

Middle class and *nouveau riche* women decided that sewing was beneath them and subcontracted the task.

Seamstresses and tailors were working overtime and, interestingly enough, determining fashion. They decided what clothes people would wear and what those clothes should look like.

Men's fashions eventually stabilized probably because by the time the Industrial Revolution was fully established, making money was the thing, not scaring the hell out of people with weird outfits and guys stopped wearing hats with feathers and took up trousers. Actually trousers became the standard for men long before the Industrial Revolution because long togas limited a man's mobility in battle and work. Women were forced to stay in dresses precisely because they limited her mobility and confirmed her fourth class status (behind men, boy children and livestock).

Over time, the concept that a woman was a person started to creep into the public consciousness and the idea started to find expression in clothes. Not men's clothes but women's clothes.

Up to the nineteenth century more or less, fashion was primarily used by women to snag a provider and that effort proved to be reasonably successful. Slowly but surely, as the steely grip on women's identity started to loosen, women began wearing clothes for their own reasons.

Variety started to appear.

Money was being spent – big money.

At first women started to wear clothes that were a little more "liberating". I didn't say not confining, but liberating. Making a statement. This is me! At last women were being able to communicate to the world and express themselves in some manner and the vehicle for that expression was/is through fashion.

Hence the variety of clothes for women since that was almost the only thing that women could do to express their uniqueness. Men seem to have more of a herd mentality and tend to look a lot alike and being the "superior" beings they don't need to be very unique.

In any case, women started demanding clothes that they wanted to wear and they had the bucks to back it up.

With the Industrial Revolution in full swing, some Moguls, males of course, realized that there was money to be made from women's desire to be unique and fashionable. Demand was way outstripping supply. Something had to be done.

Done it was. The Moguls built factories devoted to making clothes, primarily clothes for women with money.

What about the "working class" women?

Pretty much screwed fashion wise until Sears and Montgomery Ward invented their catalogues.

Explosion!

"Common folk" could now buy clothes from a catalogue at a price they could afford!

The seamstress working in a sweatshop could actually buy something she was making.

What were the rich, the *nouveau riche* and the wannabe rich going to do? Suddenly one could not differentiate one class from another (fashion snobs say they can but they really can't, they're making it up).

A new job was created: Fashion Designers. Those folks, all men of course, worked hard at creating fashion trends as fast as they could. Hopefully, faster than Sears could print the catalogue.

Bustles, hobble skirts and a whole mess of stuff came and went.

We are now in the 21st century and find that what was once a means for women to communicate has been co-opted by the Complex into a money making scheme that actually tries to subvert her desire to express her uniqueness.

Oh well.

Very few things elicit as much passion among women as clothes. A woman may say to herself: "I am (plain, dumb, fat, flat-chested, a wallflower, un-cool, etc.) and if I wear that outfit I will be (insert the antonym of the previous descriptor)."

I doubt that very many ladies say that out loud, but actions indicate that the thought is there.

The fact that none of those deprecating adjectives are even remotely true or accurate is totally beside the point. Since the time we lived in caves women and men have projected onto clothes the supernatural power of transmutation. They transfer the qualities that they would like to be onto the clothes with the presumption that if those clothes are worn that they will assume those qualities.

She says: "That blouse and skirt is sooo coool!"

He says: "I like the cut of that jacket, it's powerful"

The thing that's fascinating is that they are absolutely correct. That skirt and blouse is cool. That jacket is powerful and when we wear the garments the response we get from those who see us confirm that our sense of style was correct. Of course, it's not always clear whether the response we get is accurate or that the power of the advertising is screening out unwanted data.

The screening probably accounts for fashion faux pas.

"My God, what is she thinking?"

Let's have a little quiz here.

If a lady looks at herself in the mirror and describes what she sees by using some deprecating adjective, she is:

1. Making an accurate assessment
2. Near sighted
3. Under the control of the femininity concept.
4. Igor's lady

You answered 1?

ARRRP!

WRONG

I'm sorry, the correct answer is 3. You'll have to go home with no money, but we enjoyed having you. Let's have a round of applause for...

The Clothing Moguls know all about the feminine rule and have a big hand in trying to define what it means. So do the fashion mag Moguls, the celeb mag Moguls, the Red Carpet organizers, the celebrities themselves (although some of them have a special kind of weirdness), the raw material manufacturing Moguls (cloth, thread, buttons, that kind of stuff) and any other Mogul that you can think of.

Women's clothing is BIG business. About 100 billion bucks a year or 11 million an hour or about three dollars a day for every female in the United States – boggles the mind!

Those figures exclude shoes which, if added in, might double the numbers.

Shoes, like clothes, are designed for utility, attraction and image projection. Utility designs mean that you can actually walk around in them without damaging your foot and not becoming overly tired. These shoes generally have a short heel (less than two and a half inches), good arch support and plenty of room for toes.

Good idea but generally rejected by women who have been taught to believe the lie that tall is better than short and that higher heels make their legs, butt and foot look...what? Sexier.

Hogwash!

When's the last time a man actually noticed your shoes?

I'll bet he notices your butt even if you're barefoot.

Higher heels perpetuate the myth of female helplessness (some call it feminine) by making it difficult for the wearer to move around and damages the foot, ankles and back.

Not too bright.

Not only that, the design and fascination with shoes began with men when they had to have heels on their shoes to keep their feet in the stirrups when riding a horse. Good heels, no falling off. Hence the expression "well heeled". Also, about the time men were wearing all those weird outfits, some men took to wearing long pointed shoes to show, supposedly, that they had long penises. Long pointed shoes for women; what the hell does that mean?

Handbags or purses are another item that hampers a woman's mobility and freedom. They were originally designed to carry stuff around but a lot of stuff of yore is no longer required and handbags have become repositories for all kinds of items. Lists, gum wrappers, change at the bottom, tampons, prophylactics, makeup, another bag for credit cards and folding money, telephones, etc., etc. All important but are they necessary to have on your person at all times?

Further, fashion requirements invented by the Complex dictate that the purse, bag or whatever you call that monstrosity match other items of your clothing and therefore the contents must be shifted as required. As a result, from time to time some items are forgotten and the lady is forced to admit that her credit card, checkbook, driver's license or whatever was left in her other purse. Embarrassing and perpetuating the myth that women are stupid.

Think about it. Phones are thin, credit cards are thin, folding money is thin, change should be deposited in a jar at the end of each day and the rest of the stuff could fit in a very small bag or pocket.

Pocket?

Heaven forbid that we should design clothes for women that have utility as well as style and would allow the lady the use of both hands, have freedom of movement and won't destroy her shoulders.

Heaven forbid that ladies should decide that using pockets is more important than sporting their shapes.

I don't know how to break it to you but I already know you have an ass, a waist, tits and probably fine thighs. Why don't you show me the beauty of your mind?

Obviously I'm just a dumb pig.

The clothing Moguls aren't dumb, are working hard at perpetuating the idea that you must look feminine and have made a science of convincing every one of us that a certain collection of colored material, thread, buttons, ribbon, whatever, assembled in a certain way will project a certain image.

They are absolutely right!

They invented the image, assembled the accouterments and we buy into it.

Damn they're good!

It's like they're the Borg from *Star Trek*: "Resistance is futile!"

Unfortunately errors occur.

"It looked better on the rack."

How many times has that been said?

Of course it looks better on the rack or manikin or advertisement, it wasn't designed for YOU.

It was designed statistically. That is, it was designed for an average configuration (bust size, waist size, shoulder width, etc.). You probably don't conform to any of those measurements (I'm not sure anyone does), but in most cases it's close enough. When the misfit between you and the garment are what you perceive to be acceptable, you wear it; when those differences are not acceptable, it looked better on the rack.

The tolerance for acceptability varies with the type of clothing.

Utilitarian clothing: loose tolerances.

Image projection clothing: tighter tolerances

Attraction clothing: gang busters!

Unfortunately no matter how unreasonable, illogical and sometimes downright mean it may be, how one wears clothes effects ones self-perception and the perception of you by others.

Cultural truism: if you wear baggy clothes, you will feel baggy and others will treat you as if you were a bag.

Is that true or are we taught to believe it is true?

Think about it.

Don't think about logically, that's a waste of time; think about it emotionally — does it *feel* right that you are a bag because of the clothes you wear?

The forces at work to try to get us to conform to what acceptable standards exist <u>at a particular time</u> are powerful indeed.

We look back sixty years at poodle skirts, petticoats, bobby socks of even further back to hoop skirts or other fashions worn by women and men and think of them as quaint or downright stupid but fervently believe that the fashions of today are correct.

Will our fashions today be viewed as quaint in twenty years?

Absolutely!

Does that make you think that maybe, just maybe, you are paying too much attention to your clothes and spending too much money and wasting too much time?

Hmmmm.

There are, however, other tolerances that are more difficult to quantify.

"It just doesn't look right. What do you think, Honey?"

ALERT! ALERT!

OOOGAH... OOOGAH!!

ATTENTION ALL HANDS. THERE IS WEIRDNESS LOOSE AND COMING IN FAST AT THREE O'CLOCK!!!

The lady loves you but she has asked an unanswerable question and your ship is about to be sunk!

If you ladies think that there is a better explanation for her to ask that kind of perverse question than the continuous hammering on her to make her insecure, I'll be glad to entertain the idea.

per·verse *adj.* Cranky; peevish.

Ladies, why do you insist on setting up your man like that?

How is he supposed to know what *right* is?

I suggest, madam, that you don't know what *right* is either because some advertisement, some image, some Mogul's set of words snuck into your head and stomped the shit out of your good sense.

That kind of scenario draws laughter when posed by a comedian, but it doesn't bode well for relationships or equality.

It's weird.

On the other hand, is it silly that women have more clothes and shoes and other stuff than men?

Look mister man, all of your clothes come in four colors, black, brown, blue and gray, so you need two pairs of shoes plus maybe some work shoes and kick-back shoes. Women's clothes come in an almost infinite number of colors, hence lots of shoes.

Deal with it!

Is it fair?

Who cares?

Is there a con job being perpetrated by the Complex? You bet!

Can you do anything about it?

Don't know, you figure it out.

Sometime along the way bold and bright colors were deleted from men's wardrobes. A man wearing a bright red suit to a board meeting is not acceptable. In my mind, that's unfortunate, but that's the rule for menfolk. Maybe if we lightened up a little on men's fashions, we would have more fun and be less rigid about everything.

Who knows?

Ask Bill Gates or Steve Jobs.

Anyhow, somewhere out there is the perfect outfit that will fit the image of the "ideal" woman that exists only in a lady's head and placed there by the Complex and social pressure. The image seems to be somewhat vague, apparently changes over time and varies from individual to individual. Because the image is vague and changing, the usable life of a particular outfit is limited and new outfits are required in the vain attempt to achieve the unattainable goal.

Good for the women's clothing Moguls, bad for the budget.

"I wore that outfit the last time we went to Gloria's house".

Women have the power to demand respect in the fashion marketplace by not opening their purses and every fashion Mogul shivers at the thought that they might exercise that option.

Wear what you want to. Change styles and colors if you want to or accessorize the same outfits. Do whatever you want but don't be conned into believing that the centuries old behavior dictating that you must wear the right clothes to snag a provider is still valid today – it is not. It is not because you don't need a provider. You need a partner.

Don't be conned into believing that what you wear is you. The fact is that it is the other way around. You are you, your clothes only protect you from the elements, reveal who you are and glorify your essence.

Sometimes you just want to have fun.

Cool!

Here's a suggestion. If you can afford to shop at Sax or some other "high fashion" place, don't. Save some money, invest it in stock or bonds, get control of your life and don't let some foolish fashion person dictate your life.

Remember that the requirement that fashion must change with the seasons was invented by the Complex to get your money – you can choose not to comply.

Think about it.

Also mister manly man, think about this: a woman's continual quest to find the "right" outfit for the right time is an expression of creativity, flexibility and awareness. If us pigs were more creative, flexible and aware we might do a much better job of solving the incredible problems that confront us all.

Five

The Worms Crawl in, the Worms Crawl Out...

It is rude, crude and socially unacceptable to ask a woman her age.

Weird.

Actually it's not so weird, it's the attractiveness corollary to the male/female rule.

Not too long ago, say 70 to 100 years ago, being old was kind of cool. If you lived past sixty, you were admired and recognized for your toughness, resilience and wisdom.

Most old people were women.

Probably still is that way.

I don't know.

Hmmm.

Old equals toughness, resilience and wisdom.

Most old people were/are women.

Hmmm.

I mentioned this apparent fact (?) to some folks and I got all kinds of "answers".

"Women don't have to work like men do." "Women are taken care of and protected." "Etc."

Baloney!

That crap may have been true in olden times but now? I'm not so sure.

Wasn't true then either. Have you ever tried to cook a meal in an open fireplace? Wash clothes on a washboard? Sew by candlelight? Milk cows every morning before sunup all while caring for your rug rats and submitting to your husband's sexual demands?

For whatever reason, a woman's life expectancy is longer than a man's.

This is supposed to be a good thing, so why do so many women want to pretend they're not old?

Anti-aging (death delaying) is big business.

It's the Complex again and they know about the male/female rule.

This is how it seems to work.

At some point in a woman's life, usually around thirty, she decides that the signs of aging are starting to appear. What those signs are seems to depend on the woman. For some, it's a little sag here, a little bulge there; for others it's a wrinkle here a crease there. Whatever the signs, she detects something that seems to be different than the image she has of herself when she was nineteen or twenty-five or whatever — what she remembers herself to look like. The important thing to note here is that we are dealing with two very subjective variables. One is memory and the other is vision.

Memory is always a problem because what we remember is not necessarily what was. That's why we are always a little surprised when we look at our high school photos. We remember what we looked like but we don't remember looking like that.

"Don't show those pictures, honey. I look so dorky."

The image that we have of our youth has been massaged by feelings, some good and some bad, and our high school picture does not reflect what we remember looking like. The reality has been replaced by what we wish we had looked like.

Since our memory is unreliable, particularly when it comes to personal stuff, the Complex spends a lot of cash trying to supplant the last vestige of reality that exists in our heads with an image of their own.

They generally succeed.

The other problem is vision. Remember that I said that what we see depends on how well our eyes and brains work? The same thing happens in this context. We "see" what we want to "see". The eyes may be working fine, but the processor, the brain, may be saying:

"Uh, uh, honey. You were never that dopey."

You know you are thirty. Therefore you cannot be youthful looking. Therefore every conceivable "flaw" is examined to confirm that you are aging.

The perfect circular argument.

It matters not at all that the "flaw" was once viewed as cute, now it is an abomination.

Call 1-800-555-DOLT to sign up for a Botox party today. Operators are standing by...

Then there's the chronology thing. As a child, she and every other child in the world, was and is convinced that someone over thirty was OLD. In the 1960s it was a mantra: "You can't trust anyone over thirty".

Why the arbitrary age of thirty was chosen, I had no idea. Why not thirty-two or twenty-eight?

I had no idea.

Anyhow, thirty seems to be some kind of deeply rooted mystical milestone like Halley's comet, a solar eclipse, a Bar Mitzvah or something.

I decided to investigate.

I read history books, math books and a couple of history of math books. What I found out kind of goes like this:

Back in the old cave days, the folks weren't too big on time. They spent their days hunting and surviving. Eventually things changed. I don't know, bad weather, too many little folks or whatever, so a bunch of them set up camp along some river.

Things were tough for a while until someone (probably any one of the women who were tending after children) discovered that the seeds they were spitting all over the place produced plants. After a couple of years the women got organized and started farming.

Growing their own food cut down on the need to hunt so much and some dudes discovered fishing and pretty soon things got pretty comfy. Suddenly things were pretty good, plenty of food, a lot of corpulent women and a lot of free time.

A lot of free time meant that they started thinking.

Free time provides time to think. Thinking
produces innovation. Innovation produces change
and change eliminates free time until what was
change is now normal and free time returns.

-- Me.

Now that they didn't have to devote all of their energy to hunting to survive, a lot of them stared noticing things. They noticed that the sun came up and went down pretty regularly, that the moon did the same thing and the river as well. Of course the women were way ahead of the guys on that one because of their menstrual cycle.

With time on their hands, the menfolk used their free time to form armies and plot on ways to takeover nearby villages.

That's the manly thing to do. Stupid maybe but these guys weren't bright.

Oh, I forgot. We still do the same; must be that masculine rule.

Anyhow, warfare was fun as long as you were winning, but there was some discontent. First off, not everybody survived the battles, which pissed off some of the ladies who were left without a provider. They had to move out to the edge of the village and latch on to a farmer or become hookers.

The other group who was pissed was the farmer and hunter/fisher guys and gals. The boss of the whole group now had a standing army that had to be fed and clothed which meant that part of what they harvested or trapped had to go to the army.

Tax.

Another part of having an army was Research and Development (R&D) to produce bigger, better and more powerful weapons. Pure research was pretty much frowned on just like today. After a while, lean times came and the boss, let's call him Igor, had trouble feeding his army.

He called a meeting.

"This is lion shit!" He said

The crowd gasped.

"We've got to find a way to increase production. We've raped and pillaged all over the place and all we get is refugees and pregnant women. I've got to find a way to go further."

There was a lot of murmuring and shifting around.

Finally a voice at the back of the crowd spoke up.

"My name is Little Igor. I think we have to figure a way to predict when the river comes up and when the seasons change so we can plant and hunt more efficiently."

"That's a long-range solution, "Igor shouted, "I need an answer for now!"

"But if we can do what I suggest we can be ten times more powerful later. I've got this guy, Gates 1st, who has an idea…"

"Is there something wrong with your ears? Me Igor. Me Director. Me no like innovation. Only weapons."

Little Igor strode across the room and slew Igor

"I am now Igor II."

The first coup d'état.

Igor II gave Gates 1st a government contract to determine when the best time to plant and harvest crops.

Pretty straightforward assignment except for a couple of small details like counting and recording time.

Let's assume for a minute that you are Gates 1st and there is no arithmetic, very little written language and you are essentially asked to invent time.

How would you do it?

Dah, dah dah dah. Dah dah dah dah dah dah!

(Theme from *Jeopardy*, jeez I thought everyone knew that)

Time's up! You lose.

Tough assignment but Gates 1st wasn't about to be put down.

The first thing he did was round up as many experts as he could find. None of these guys were exactly what you would call conformists – bad haircuts, skinny, game players and some old guys. If you think gals were excluded you are mistaken – you know seers, oracles, old crones and the like – besides they had the rhythm of life.

Once he had his team assembled, the first order of business was to invent writing. Not the fancy stuff that came after the invention of religion, but the simple stuff mostly pictures on clay.

Once everyone agreed on the code (that's what writing is), the next thing was to compile all the collective knowledge.

Some guys had noticed that if you looked at the shadow of a rock on the sand, that shadow would appear at a slightly different place each sun-up, but after a bunch of sun-ups the pattern would repeat.

"Hey Dude, I want some of your stash. That's some bad weed."

Laughter.

"OK, OK guys, let's settle down. That's valuable information."

Gates 1st believed in inclusion.

The next order of business was to figure out a numbering system.

A lot of discussion here but they finally settled on a duodecimal system based on the number of joints on the fingers of each hand: 24. Thumbs were ignored because they only have two joints.

Then they decided that they had to figure out how many sun-ups passed before the cycle started again. They did this by making piles of 24 pebbles (all the joints of both hands); each rock would represent one sun-up. They made piles of the pebbles and when a pile reached 24 (eight fingers), they would start a new pile. When the shadow was back to the staring place, they had collected 15 piles of 24 pebbles or 360 plus five pebbles. A lot more discussion was held because no one liked the five-finger thing and they didn't know what to do with the extra pebbles.

While that was going on, the druggie in the back of the room yelled out:

"Hey dudes, I took these cool pebbles and made piles. Instead of eight fingers, 24 pebbles, I used one hand (twelve finger joints) and the total number of rocks is the same!"

Twelve piles of thirty rocks.

Everybody liked that and they assigned the guy in the back to further subdivide the day into equal parts. Since he was hung up on the twelve thing, it seemed like a good idea to use all of his finger joints subdivide a day, sunup to sunup. Depending on the month of the year they would be off a little but nobody seemed to mind.

They gave the divisions names: One joint, one hour; 24 joints, one day; 30 pebbles (days), one month; 12 months one year.

A particularly nerdy guy in the front of the room who was into watching the cycle of the stars chose the first month of the year. He decided that when a particular star was directly overhead should be the beginning of the year.

The next thing Gates 1st and his crew did was to build an obelisk in a strategically located spot. With the obelisk's shadow, Gates 1st was able to draw a semicircle in the sand, which he divided into equal parts…

Time and a clock by which to measure it was born.

Gates 1st presented his data to Igor II and got a big bonus.

Now everyone knew when to plant and when to harvest and production increased tenfold.

Of course, it didn't take too long for everybody to figure out that there were five days left over, but…

Let's party!!!

Years later, the Romans still couldn't figure out what to do with the extra five days so they named the extra time after Jupiter and…

Let's party!!!

The Christians eventually came and named the time Christmas and…

Let's party!!!

Some folks in different parts of the world came up with different systems but the idea of a 24-hour day pretty much took hold. Not particularly accurate but close enough and easy to use (kind of like *Windows*). The months were originally 30 days each, but later on various Emperors changed them to suit their political or egocentric needs.

"You said that there were women on the team."

Yup. Esmeralda spoke up at one of the meetings:

"Wait a minute here," the idea of time caught on fast, "you guys are always yapping about the sun. What about the moon?"

"What about it?"

"Well dummy, the moon's cycle is pretty close to my cycle. So we can watch the moon and know when it's best to make babies. What about that?"

"OK. The sun is the guy's thing and the moon is the gal's thing."

Esmeralda saw an opportunity and she and her buddies, the seers, the crones, and the mystics, grabbed it.

A HUGE public relations mistake.

For a long time women were associated with the eerie darkness of night and by extension a lot of bad things. You know, witches and that kind of stuff. Pretty soon women were blamed for almost everything.

Gods pissed off?

Sacrifice a woman, preferably a thin virgin – she's worthless anyhow.

No sons?

Woman's fault.

People acting weird?

Witches.

Husband strays?

Hussies.

Eve and the apple?

Hmmm.

Anyhow, now that everyone could measure time, some other things were noticed. One was that people lived about 35 to 40 years and that after about thirty, very few women had babies. Why, nobody knew. The exhaustion factor probably played a part. Those women had been hunting, breeding, cooking, tending and living in nearly impossible conditions for their whole lives. Probably just worn out. For whatever reason, a woman's usefulness as breeding stock was diminished and she was relegated to lesser importance in the clan.

The age of thirty years was chosen as THE milestone because of its significance to the 360 day thing and the concept of time.

Thirty-two or twenty-eight aren't nearly as neat.

You may have noticed that age is only tangentially related to the magical thirty number. Its real significance was the value of a woman to the clan as breeding stock.

You would think that we would have gotten over that prehistoric mentality by now.

I guess not.

I turned thirty and hardly noticed.

My wife turned thirty and it was a big deal.

Weird.

It is a big deal!

"I'm going to be twenty-nine forever!"

Turning thirty is a huge milestone for a lot of women.

I threw a surprise birthday party for my wife on her thirtieth birthday and sent out invitations styled as death notices: The death of her twenty-ninth year. I requested that the men wear black armbands and the women wear as little as possible. A couple of our friends thought she had really died, which was a little strange but verified the effectiveness of the message. I had a big cake made in the fashion of a coffin and I decorated our house with black wreaths and other wake paraphernalia. When she entered the house and was surprised by our friends, I had a dirge played as we escorted her to where the cake was laying in state.

The party was a huge success and lasted well into the next morning.

No one questioned the fact that it was an important milestone nor the symbolism of the wake motif, it's culturally accepted. Twenty-one is also an important milestone, but it has more to do with legality than anything else.

At thirty, a lot of women start paying attention to the fact that they are aging. They may have noticed signs before, but they weren't thirty yet so it was OK. At thirty the same signs are suddenly not OK.

I can understand why, for women, the aging thing was important concern in Igor's time because once you couldn't breed, they set you out on flat rock to be eaten by wolves, but now…

It's weird.

Men cope with the age thing in just about the same way they cope with anything else: a shrug.

The Moguls have tried to develop products for men, like hair dyes, hair transplants, exercise equipment and other stuff, but that market is marginal at best.

Most men don't give a shit.

It's the rule.

Aging for most men is a physical inconvenience and firmly believe in the saying; "Old age and cunning will overcome youth and ambition every time."

Older men view younger men with disdain and chuckle at their youthful exuberance.

Older women envy and sometimes fear younger women.

Men just get older and kind of enjoy it.

Women get older and pretend they are not.

Men use age as a good excuse for being really sloppy and keeping that old shirt.

Women use age as an excuse to buy more stuff.

Here's an example for you.

I work as a checkout clerk for a large retail chain and one of my responsibilities is to ask for identification if a purchase is being made with a credit card. I will frequently make silly comments to the male customers when I look at the picture on the identification.

"Who is this young guy in this picture?"

Not one single man complains at my banter.

I dare not say the same thing to a woman.

Weird.

I don't know for sure, but it's probable that some "brilliant" psychiatrists, sociologists, anthropologists or some kind of social scientists have written countless complicated tomes on the subject of women and their apprehension of aging. If they have, they probably discussed genetics, culture, brain construction and a bunch of other stuff – all wrong.

By now, of course, we know the why of the weirdness. It is an obsession with the rule that says that a woman is female; female implies softness, pliancy, naiveté, attractive, etc; it is presumed that youthfulness seems to satisfy those requirements. Thus not-young negates all of those attributes. The Complex knows this and keep everybody all stirred up. If they didn't a bunch of products won't sell.

Of course the products designed to make one appear youthful, will be more expensive. It's more expensive because…

You're worth it!

You guessed it; I'm going to launch into some extreme examples of what happens when youth is excessively venerated

Let's start out slow.

Facial creams.

As far as I can determine there are three kinds of creams: one to cleanse (ad-speak for cleaning), one to moisturize (add-speak for adding oil to your skin) and wrinkle suppressors.

The cleansing creams are designed to wash away all the crap that you put on your face in the morning, remove blackheads and minimize blemishes (a blemish is ad-speak for pimple). Most of the Moguls don't want you to use soap on your face because it supposedly dries out your skin (soap doesn't the detergents in "soap" do) and soap has a lower profit margin because it is considerably less expensive. One soap manufacturer advertises that it has moisturizer in it to combat that particular ploy.

Using facial creams or other kinds of body lotions isn't particularly weird, expecting it to keep you "youthful" is, but what the heck, if it makes you feel better, go for it. Besides, none of that stuff is particularly harmful.

I've got a problem with wrinkle suppressors because they don't work. If you notice, somewhere in the advertising there is a phrase that says in effect: "Minimizes the appearance of wrinkles." Very clever ad-speak because you don't know whether they are talking about something that is about to appear or something that looks like.

You know the drill. At some point you notice lines from the corner of your mouth to the edge of your nose or little lines at the corner of your eyes.

Panic. Wrinkles are unacceptable.

The fact is that if you are thirty, those little muscles have been exercised about 31 million times and in the next thirty years will be exercised another 31 million times.

You ought to be surprised that your eyes haven fallen out by now.

Oh. Wait a minute.

Wrinkles are caused by muscle action.

Stop the muscle action and wrinkles will stabilize.

Let's all run out and get Botulinum Toxin Type A (Botox) a poison derived from *Clostridium Botulinum,* which causes botulism.

I don't care what you say. If you are so obsessed with the natural emergence of wrinkles, which in some way threaten the vision of yourself, that you want to inject poison in your body, you might be weird.

Ladies that's weird behavior.

Your sisters have spent centuries trying to establish the fact that you have a mind, that you are not fourth-class, that you are intellectually exciting and that you deserve to be on equal footing with the rest of society (men) and all you can do is shoot crap in your face?

Weird.

As weird as using Botox may be, it's not permanent and there seem to be no lasting side effects. I'm sure that someone, somewhere, will figure out a way to abuse the stuff and end up with a permanently frozen expression on her face that she will carry to the grave, but that historic event is yet to come.

"Why does Aunt Caroline always look like she's been goosed?"

"Be quiet Johnny, and don't ask rude questions!"

Some quests to reach that unattainable image are a little more permanent.

Plastic Surgery.

Interesting name for a medical procedure to say the least. I suppose it comes from the *Plastic Man* comics or something like that.

Wrong!

It comes from the Greek word *plastikos*, which means to mold or give form.

There are a couple of things that annoy me about the current popular perception of Plastic Surgery.

The first is that there seems to be a perception that this particular branch of medicine is almost wholly devoted to the business of changing the configuration of women so that they can achieve their "ideal". Not true. Most of the practitioners of Plastic Surgery concentrate on real disfigurement caused by burns, accidents, birth defects, war wounds and even the effects of other surgical procedures like mastectomies.

Plastic Surgeons are not big on the hack and slash techniques utilized by most surgeons and often have to step in and repair disfiguring results from surgeries. These problems often occur as a result of emergency situations where time is of the essence to save the patient's life.

As an example, my son ran into a pole while riding his bike in the neighborhood. As a result of the collision, he slashed his eyelid rather badly. Instead of taking him to an ER, I took him to a Plastic Surgeon who repaired the tear and left no scar. It is probable that the result of an emergency room surgeon would have left him with a drooping eyelid. The repair would have been made but the technique used may have provided different results.

I am of the opinion that if one has to have surgery on a particularly visible part of one's body, one should have a Plastic Surgeon do the cutting and closing since they are concerned with how the skin and muscles will come back together rather than just getting at the organ or malignancy.

Important work, Plastic Surgery.

The second thing that annoys me is that the specialty got a bad rap in 1990 from a report issued by Connie Chung overemphasizing the health risks that certain breast implants had on women who received them. It turns out that the whole report was essentially unfounded and it was subsequently proven that there were no discernible health risks from the use of this device. Those facts didn't matter and millions of dollars changed hands because of the worldwide class-action suit.

Proving once again that…

Image (perception) is much more important than substance.

The Plastic Surgeons got stuck with the image of tit surgeons, Dow Corning went bankrupt, thousands lost their jobs and the Media Moguls went unscathed. To my knowledge, Ms. Chung has never admitted to her sloppy reporting.

Like I said before, Plastic Surgery is important stuff but the profession's image is no match for the mighty female rule and its distortions.

Back to cosmetic surgery.

Let's start with simple stuff.

Rhinoplasty – nose jobs.

Rhinoplasty is important stuff if you are born with a nose that's squished up against your head with the nostrils pointed straight ahead like a pig's; or you lose it in a car accident; or have it cut up in some grotesque fashion; or broken so it isn't straight, but a bump on the ridge?

I don't know.

Maybe a really big bump.

The size of the bump is determined by the individual comparing his or her current appearance to an image that they have in their head.

I suppose that I could accept an individual deciding that their nose just looks like crap.

Relative to what?

Relative to other people pointing and laughing or looking at with revulsion or…

"Hey dude, your nose looks like crap. Get it fixed or wear mask or something."

I would say those conditions merit some thought on the subject.

However, changing the configuration of your nose to make you *feel* better about yourself or to make you more *attractive* is weird.

It's WEIRD and dangerous.

It's the cosmetic surgery Moguls using other elements of the Complex's advertising to convince you that you shouldn't look like you.

Breast augmentation is the same drill. If you have a so-so personality, having big boobs is not going to land you Prince Charming, but it may land you a guy who has a breast fixation and something strange going on with his mother.

Don't you think that you ought to be judged by the content of your character rather than the size of your tits?

Demand it!

Also the true measure of a man starts at the neck and goes up not by his abs, butt or size of his penis.

Just a side comment here: a lot of models have small breasts and command six figure salaries, exotic dancers – not so much.

Is there a connection there?

Hmmmm.

Breast *reduction* makes sense; less strain on your back and you can find clothes on the rack that actually fit.

Face lift?

Someone is beating your common sense into a pulp.

I suppose, if you are in "show biz", you can rationalize that you won't get any parts if you start to "age". Unfortunately there is that little thing called talent that keeps cropping up regardless of your face.

Here's an interesting note on some trends. Some practitioners are so obsessed with getting your money that they have adapted the use of lasers to attract customers who are afraid of being cut. The reconfiguration only lasts a few years (duh, no face lift lasts forever) so there is a built-in recurring market. They claim no side or long lasting effects, but then no one knows for sure.

Another trend is to do work on younger and younger girls.

"Judy, honey, your father and I have noticed that your nose is a little different and we decided to treat you to some cosmetic procedures so you will be more popular when you get into high school."

Hooray, Hooray! Let's have the kid sliced, diced and bobbed before she is finished growing. Oh, by the way, Judy's a minor and really doesn't have a vote.

"Judy can always say no."

Yeah, right. With parents like that – bordering on the insane – I don't think so!

Let me get this straight.

Parents give their child a good shellacking for cutting off her little sisters hair – abuse.

Parents have their child's face or body surgically reconfigured – not abuse.

Weird and dangerous.

I want to tell you about a segment I saw in the *View* the other day. If you don't know what the *View* is, I'll tell you. It's a very popular TV talk show wherein four or five ladies sit around a table and have a more or less unscripted bull session discussing topics of the day and guests are invited who are pimping their latest endeavors.

Recently, one entire hour show was devoted to the latest and greatest Plastic Surgery (cosmetic surgery actually) methods. One of the newest techniques has to do with orthodontia. The theory is that reconfiguring a child's jaw or mouth in general will prevent that child from aging "poorly".

That whole concept is so weird that even choice obscenities won't make it go away.

Anyhow, the person who is pimping this procedure claims to be able to tell how a child will look by the time they are forty if the procedure is not performed. To prove their point they use similar software developed to assist in the search for missing children and the reconstruction of sculls by forensic experts. They take the child's picture, digitize it, run the program and show how the child's looks change as she/he ages.

Pretty neat, huh?

Are you insane????

Got to calm down.

This pimp is trying to get you to spend money and put your child through some procedure based on a facial recognition program. Does it ever occur to you that the program may have been written to the specifications designed by the pimp? That is, the pimp hires some software outfit to produce aging images starting with a baseline (the child's digitized photograph) and then progressing through the child's aging process and finally showing what the child will look like at some older age if you do not perform the procedure. The pimp's specifications specifically describe the images that the pimp wants, not what really is going to happen.

"Hey Mr. Singh, write me a facial recognition program that shows a distended upper lip for a child that has an overbite."

"How much distension, Ms. Pimp?"

"Oh, I don't know, two or three millimeters ought to do it."

That's the way it works, sports fans.

Am I trying to say that orthodontia is a bad thing?

No.

What I am saying is that some software programmer in New Delhi was hired to make this crap up. That's what software does, it simulates reality; it is _not_ reality.

Will your child look like the images presented?

No one knows!

If you believe the crap presented by the images, you are weird and you are trying your best to make your child (usually a girl child) weird.

Shame on you!

If your kid's teeth don't align correctly or has a serious overbite or whatever, go to a legitimate orthodontist and have the problem corrected; don't go to the circus.

No one, and I mean NO ONE, can predict with any degree of certainty what a person will look like in thirty years.

Period.

Besides, why are you imposing your view of "good looks" on your child when the whole concept of attractiveness will be different in thirty years?

Tattoo or pierced lip anyone?

Like I said, weird and dangerous.

"What's wrong with trying to look your best?"

Nothing, but you've got to admit that there is a significant difference between "looking your best" which implies taking what you've got and working with it, not alteration. Wearing clothes that suit you, coloring your hair or changing hairstyles for fun, exercising and eating food that is commensurate with your body are all "good" things but trying to stop the inevitable *superficial* aging process through the use of surgery or "magic" lotions can become obsessive and by definition weird.

Also, the concepts that young is "good" and old is "bad", that fat is "bad" and thin is "good" or that pretty is "good" and plain is "bad" are part of our current culture and trying to achieve those "goals" can be enormously difficult, frustrating and expensive.

Most of that pressure is on women.

Unfair!

Here is a quote from Jacqueline Bisset for you to think about:

Character contributes to beauty. It fortifies a woman as her youth fades.

Six

Who Started this Mess Anyhow?

Many of the mores (rules) invented thousands of years ago involving women and men and their position in society are still in vogue. Those mores were developed to assure the survival of our species when human life was very precarious. They have been modified and cleverly disguised somewhat but the basic premise still persists that holds that a woman needs a provider to survive and that she is valued only for her appearance which will attract a male and breeding will occur. Those mores persist in spite of the fact that virtually none of the conditions that required their invention still exist.

A significant reason for the persistence of the female/male rule and its corollaries is that we confuse biology with culture.

Biologically there can be no doubt that we are physically designed to be able to procreate, but with humans there is a little hitch – we want to do it all the time. Not only that, we intellectualize about the activity. We have fantasies, we plan, we seek mechanical or medical assistance, we buy costumes, we do all sorts of things to get laid or at least experience the pleasure of the act. We spend a considerable amount of time and money to achieve that end and it seems to matter not at all that sometimes (often?) the experience is not as satisfying as we had imagined it was going to be, but we keep on plugging.

Being sexy, we are told, is a highly desirable state for males and females.

Men generally have no training and therefore no idea how to be sexy. After all, the rule asserts that men are supposed to be the predators, so why worry?

Women are taught at a very early age by role models and the society at large how to be sexy. After all, the rule asserts that women are supposed to be passive and snag a provider, so if you've got it flaunt it.

What a pretty little girl.

Of course, what sexy is and is not varies with time, culture and prevailing attitudes.

What is sexy for a young woman/man is not the same for an older woman/man; what is sexy in Germany is not the same in Kenya; what is sexy for a porno-queen is not the same for a CEO; etc.

Sexiness is determined, to a very large degree, by the beholder.

Remember? To a man, a woman is beautiful if he loves her and she returns the affection.

We are told that the sex drive is an important part of our genetic makeup.

Maybe so, but it is not the only factor and that "drive" manifests itself in almost as many ways as there are people.

I would suggest that the real factor in the "drive" is for companionship, mutual affection, mutual respect and optimism – sex (the verb) is merely a side effect.

A fun, exhilarating, relaxing, temporarily meaningful side effect, but a side effect never the less.

We, as a species, don't survive well alone. Physically we are less strong than many other species. Intellectually, however, we are champions. Along with our ability to think we have compassion, empathy, communication skills and a need to care for and be cared for by other humans. We even want to care for other species like cats, dogs, horses, etc.

Sounds like "feminine" characteristics to me.

Is it possible that the values associated with the rule are so wrong that we've got it backwards?

Is it possible that "feminine" characteristics are actually more defining elements of what we are as a species?

Is it possible that "feminine" characteristics are more important to our ability to survive than those "masculine" traits like strength, aggression, analysis, etc.?

If those possibilities are correct, then the rule stating that men are masculine and women are feminine is meaningless. If those possibilities are correct then women and men are only defined by their configuration, as complex as it might be, and behavior has very little to do with defining one's gender.

However, the rule is still in force and women and men, some more than others, seem to be fascinated with their personal appearance, which has resulted in huge industries that are aware of this and work tirelessly to confuse us about our personal appearance in order to strip us of our cash. Those industries concentrate on things like PREPARATION, diets, clothes, physical configuration, etc. -- appearance things – by presenting words and images designed to create insecurity thereby making us susceptible to fleecing.

This condition affects women more than men because the rule requires that men be aggressive and women passive and therefore she should (must?) create an alluring image in order to snag a provider or at least have sex.

Assuming that my observations are correct, then the nagging question is why?

Why would women all over the world willingly subject themselves to this barrage of crap and buy into it to the tune of billions of dollars?

Why would men all over the world willingly subject themselves to the lie that presumes that they are superior and spend the rest of their lives being confronted with the fact that they are not?

The easy and incorrect answer is that human behavior is predisposed by genetics. That is, women concentrate on their appearance in order to breed and social constructs are created to facilitate that purpose.

Maybe so but that model seems to ignore that people have minds, free will and a pretty good sense of cause and effect. Also, sex is fun all by itself and a lot of people have sex with no intention whatsoever of breeding. In the extreme case, accidental impregnation occurs and many women decide to terminate the pregnancy thereby completely reversing the genetic thing.

No, genetics alone isn't it.

That is not to say that women don't want to have babies. The fact is that most women at some time in their lives want to have children but in the 21ˢᵗ century many women have a choice as to when and how many thereby muting whatever genetic predisposition might exist.

No, genetics isn't it.

So if women are not forced by genetics to behave a certain way, then the question remains: why would women all over the world willingly subject themselves to this barrage of crap and buy into it to the tune of billions of dollars?

The answer is that the revolution initiated by the Women's Movement has not been completed. The hearts and minds of the populace have not changed. All the Moguls, male and female, understand this and continually assault women with the idea that she should be sexy, radiant, lustrous, thin, smooth, etc., etc. and will do anything to continue the myth that a woman's only real function is to snag a man and breed.

Politics? Business? Sports? The Arts?

Mere dalliances. Get yourself dolled up girl and go get laid!

Lies!

Myths, lies and nonsense invented long, long ago by people who weren't too bright and it's taken us over ten thousand years to begin to understand what a huge error that was.

The first question then is how and why did this error occur?

If I know how and why, maybe there is a solution.

I read books on anthropology, theology, archeology and a whole bunch of other "ologies" as well as a lot of current stuff.

All I got was a headache ant the faint smell of horse pucky.

It turns out that with the advent of DNA analysis and the fact that there are a lot of people investigating our past, one would think that we would have an answer. Surprisingly, there are more theories than answers but I suspect that the reason for this is that no one is looking at the data from the point of view that an error was committed. Also, everyone is looking at the data from a male point of view and ignoring any contribution or leadership that females provided.

The rule even affects scientific inquiry.

To assume that males did everything is preposterous!

Oh well, since no one can seem to agree on almost anything, I guess I'll give it my best shot.

Will what I am about to say be true and accurate?

Hell, I don't know, you decide.

Gotta start at the beginning because, as you might suspect by now, I have a slightly different view than the prevailing thinking and I will present information that is common knowledge without gender bias; that is males didn't do everything.

Before I get too far, let me make it clear that I don't give a hoot about the why the hominids (us) came to be, nor am I interested in the details of the how, the fact is that we are here and that's it. If you are a religious person and are so insecure in your faith that you feel compelled to engage in endless, nonsensical arguments, which attempt to explain the "How and Why We Came to Be", then nock yourself out. If, however, your insecurity is so extreme that you feel compelled to FORCE the current brand of "How and Why We Came to Be" on everyone else, then someone should knock you out.

Enough said.

Speciation, the formation of a new species, is not a particularly unique event. Estimates have been made that put the number of species in the tens of millions, most of which are insects. That would mean that speciation occurs almost every year. The estimated number of mammals, which breed live young and must feed and care for them, is about 4,600. We are one of those guys.

There are several theories of how speciation takes place and even more speculation as to why, but environmental changes seem to be the prevalent impetus. What seems to happen is that an offspring is born with a slightly different genetic makeup and the more complex the species, the higher probability that the offspring will have a slightly different genetic makeup. That's why the DNA structure for each individual human is unique. That genetic change is transmitted to another offspring and now there are several. These new kids breed and now there is a whole bunch. None of this maters much unless some of the new guys go live somewhere else and eventually becomes isolated. Once isolated, the same process occurs and eventually the new kids become different kids and a new species emerges.

For insects, plants and simple organisms this process can be fairly rapid because each generation produces millions of offspring in very short time spans, which accounts for most of the different species being something other than mammals.

Plants, since they don't move around much, are very susceptible to climate change but migrate quite rapidly because wind, insects and birds carry their seed. Many new species of plants derived from parent plants exist thousands of miles from their origins.

For more complex organisms that don't breed as quickly, the process may take millions of years.

Here is a classic case of speciation. The genus *Pan* has two species. One is the common Chimpanzee and the other is the Bonobo or pygmy chimpanzee. It seems that about 1.5 or 2 million years ago the Congo River was formed and some of the chimps got stuck on the south side. Chimps can't swim very well so the groups remained separated. As I explained before, sure enough the guys on the south became a new species.

It is currently presumed that apes and hominids (us) come from common ancestors and Chimpanzees seem to be our closest relatives; both types I guess.

Apparently there were several brands of hominids like the Homo habilis, Homo neanderthalensis (Neanderthals), Homo erectus, etc. but we, the Homo sapiens, are the only remaining bunch.

The rest are toast.

The separation process for the new kids went something like this.

"Ethel, have you noticed that Igor and Elvira spend a lot of time standing up? What's up with that?"

"I've noticed, and they're kind of ugly, you know, their faces are funny looking."

"They are a bad influence and the forests are starting to get smaller, let's move and leave no forwarding address."

It's also possible that there were some natural cataclysms like a tornado, earthquake, volcanic eruption, ice age, global warming, etc. and the older guys weren't equipped to handle the new conditions.

So either Igor and Elvira were thrown out of the pack, or they split on their own or the natural operation of the planet created new conditions and the result was that they distanced themselves from their antecedents.

That little scenario probably occurred in many places over a long period of time, say a million years – about 65,000 generations.

Some of the exiles made it, others didn't.

Besides preferring to walk erect and being physically different than their ancestors, the Homo sapiens eventually developed two other characteristics; one is a significant flaw and the other a significant advantage.

The flaw was that they didn't have the highly tuned instincts that their ancestral animals did and the advantage was that they could reason – more or less.

Being born with instinct would mean that each new generation would know exactly what to do to survive.

Over time, probably a long time, the Homo sapiens slowly lost their instincts. Probably because their old instincts were not useful in their new environment.

Not good.

Food gathering and nest or shelter building wasn't much of a problem; child rearing was.

Let's say that Elvira had three children. She would have to live long enough to teach one of her girl children what to do with a baby.

Elvira breeds when she's fourteen and it's a girl. That girl, girl-one, would learn something as Elvira had more children and Elvira could do some coaching. At twenty-eight, Elvira's a grandmother and the two women could expand on their experience. Doesn't sound like much of a problem except that there are very few communication skills, no fire and virtually no margin for error.

Imagine living on the edge of the forest, naked, no instruction manual (instincts) and almost everything is hostile. You're not sure of what to eat because you have wandered off to a different place than your grandparents; every, and I mean every, other animal wants to eat you; if you fall down and break something, you would probably die; cut your foot on a sharp stone, it might become infected and you might die; it's cold and rainy or hot and arid and then multiply those hazards by two if you are trying to keep a three year old from wandering off.

The difference between that scenario and today's working mother is only a matter of degree and the availability of support systems.

Hence the prospects for survival are slim to none if only two Homo sapiens started out on their own with no support systems. Logically then, several Homo sapiens had to have started out together. You can go through the permutations about the division of labor required for survival on your own, but I believe that five is the minimum number – three females and two males.

One female in the pack is no good because it would take too long for her to pass on the child rearing skills and if she fell down, caught the flu or died, survival of the pack would be in serious jeopardy.

Two females would be better than one but still very risky.

Three females would be the minimum because they can share the birthing experience and learn from each other the techniques that are required in the child's first few years. At the same time the two non-mothers are available hunting food and shelter maintenance. Thus there would always be at least three and most of the time four people to obtain food for the clan of six.

In due time another child would be born and there may be two women lactating at the same time and all of the clan would be much more familiar with the whole process

The child, regardless of gender, would have to start contributing to the pack at a very young age, probably five or six.

In a fairly short time, say ten years, there may be as many as eight or nine individuals and maybe as many as six or seven contributing to food gathering, shelter maintenance and tool making.

This is a successful scenario, most clans were not successful and the ones that did succeed were fortunate indeed.

Actually, fortune probably didn't contribute as much as we may think since the expulsion process that Igor and Elvira went through was not sudden nor was it continuous. It probably started and stopped (the hominids returned to their original setting or died out), instinct did not disappear suddenly and the process took over thousands of years of trial and error.

Obviously the new Homo sapiens eventually got the hang of it and broke off contact with their ancestors completely.

Since these creatures had limited instincts, they had to use their intellect to refine their communication skills. It was essential that they learned to communicate in some fashion so one generation could transmit knowledge that they had learned to the next generation using reason to transmit information that wasn't there through instinct.

We all know that words or language is not the only method of communication; a grunt, sounds of some kind and body language works quite well for many, many species. It also works for us on a limited fashion; that's how we communicate with someone who doesn't speak our language. Body language is also important even if we speak the same language. The message is crystal clear if you try to kiss your date and she turns her cheek.

The problem was that as clans grew in number and/or they moved and/or the environment changed and simple grunts didn't cut it. Somehow the grunts had to be more specific.

Let's say a couple of folks set out to try and find some food or shelter and went over a hill and found what they were looking for. At the same time another couple went in another direction and did the same thing. When everyone returned a discussion would be held as to which way to go. The rest of the clan can't see over the hills and no one can figure out the best course of action. A lot of confusion and possibly violence. Obviously grunts and jumping up and down wasn't good enough. Somehow communication had to improve.

How the Homo sapiens invented language is not known, but I suspect that it was baby talk.

Here's the deal. An infant arrives on the scene. The mother, with her intuition and probably some instinct leftover from the early stages of separation, cares for the child and its hand reaches for something. At the same time it makes a sound, maybe an insistent sound. The mother, not knowing exactly what the child wants and trying to maintain the peace, starts handing the child objects. Eventually she hands it a stick and mimics the sound the baby uttered. The baby smiles and the word for stick is invented.

Farfetched? Maybe, but the mother was probably around fourteen, fifteen or younger, not a rocket scientist and operated at an intellectual level much similar to the child's.

Look around your house and see if that isn't pretty close. What mother doesn't know a tired cry from an annoyed cry, a hungry cry or some cries that just don't make any sense?

Another, hugely important event was taking place during this exchange: the development of empathy.

Empathy is the understanding of another person's situation, feelings and motives.

Animals don't have it because they operate on instincts and it is not required. Without instincts the new hominids had to develop empathy to learn to communicate and thus survive.

Here's a scenario. The mother is fearful, annoyed or just plain uncomfortable with the child's incessant utterances and through trial and error satisfies the child's immediate needs by handing it a stick and repeating the sound or even using a sound of her own. The baby calms, the mother relaxes and a tiny spark of empathy is established between mother and child. The process is repeated with other objects and there is some measure of success. The mother is convinced that she is communicating with the child and ignores the failures as we all do to justify our actions. Some level of language is developed between mother and child that continue throughout their lives. The language is shared with the other four members of the clan and progresses geometrically.

Of course, the correct amino acid combinations and gene arrangement (possibly FOXP2) had to be present as well.

If you don't think this is possible, consider the fact that many infant twins develop a method of communication that only they can understand. The technical term for this is idioglossia. No reason the same process can't be extrapolated to the mother.

Another thing that we all know is that aside from the obvious physical differences between men and women there are also brain differences – subtle perhaps, but differences just the same. These differences have only recently been scientifically confirmed. A couple of the differences have to do with communication skills and emotional processing.

All this means is that females tend to have more of their brain available for language than men and that females have a better ability to relate and express their feelings as well as a better ability to bond and connect with others.

You already knew that? Well now you've got scientific data to back it up.

Anyhow, the process of developing language took a long time and went through many permutations for a couple of reasons. One reason may have been that it is probable that not all members of the clan had the right genetic makeup for speech so the mother's information may not take. Another may have been some confusion in the passing of the sounds just like when we play "telephone", what started as one message comes out entirely different after several repetitions. This garbled communication may have caused some consternation, a little snickering and pointing as an individual struggled to make himself understood and some folks might have been hard over on the proper sounds and split from the clan altogether.

"Those dumb people keep saying 'stick' when everyone knows that 'banzi' (Swahili) is the right word."

No reason to assume that there wasn't language purist in those days, just like today.

New clan, new language.

As communication progressed, the clan now had the rudimentary ability to explain the "how to do it" of various tasks which were passed from generation to generation. Individuals that could hunt well, for instance, could teach other, younger individuals their skills. Mothers could teach mothering, toolmakers could teach their craft and so forth. In the process of teaching, behavior patterns were transmitted and a culture was formed for that particular community.

Their life style and appearance was not significantly different than the other animals except for the tool and communication things.

Communities that were successful (survived) learned teamwork, the communication skills and empathy required for teamwork, those that didn't, didn't.

Working as a team, independent of gender, the community could gather food more efficiently, protect themselves from the elements and predators better and delegate tasks to those members that exhibited talents to help the community survive.

Since the communities were relatively small in number, it is reasonable to assume that everyone had to be able to perform all the necessary tasks except birthing and care of infants, primarily nursing. Once nursing was over, the mother had to leave the children with the old people and help, or lead, in the gathering of food, a process that must be performed almost daily.

Not reasonable? Let's see. There's a community of thirty. Fifteen of those are women, eight are children and two old people. That leaves five guys to do all the hunting, tool making, predator defending or whatever. Not a very efficient distribution of skills and labor.

Mr. Trump of *The Apprentice* fame would surely have you fired.

Not reasonable? What do you think happens today?

There's a lot of workload sharing (jobs) among the genders for food gathering, shelter maintenance and tool making going on as we speak. Birthing and child rearing…not so much sharing.

As a matter of fact, women have been sharing in the workload for all of recorded history. Women have farmed, tended stores, worked in factories, fought in wars, built pyramids, etc., etc. forever. The concept that women only tended to hearth and home is based on the fact that most historical records are about the rich and well to do. Very little data on ordinary people and those folks of both genders worked their butts off. Who do you think maintained all those castles and palaces?

As time marched on and we moved into the 20th century, wealth became more evenly distributed and we had a cultural aberration which placed women's primary role as mother and housekeeper and, for reasons not clear to me and contrary to all historical data, somebody decided that arrangement is "Nature's Way".

I'll bet that somebody wasn't a woman.

Anyhow, back to the olden, golden days and mix the gender ratios any way you want, but it is obvious that women had/have to assume a significant role in food gathering (including hunting), tool making and predator defending. If they didn't the group would be toast.

They would also be toast if those "feminine" characteristics of empathy, compassion, communication, bonding, etc. weren't present.

For better or for worse, values were attached to certain behavior. For instance, fires had to be maintained, particularly if the community had not figured out how to start a fire. Thus, if an individual doused the fire, that act would be considered "bad" behavior and punishment would probably be meted out. Similarly if a young mother abandoned her nursing child, she would also be guilty of "bad" behavior. Slowly, then, mores were developed and rudimentary legal codes were established for that culture based on "good" behavior that enhanced the community's ability to survive and "bad" behavior that jeopardized the community's wellbeing.

The value associated with behavior wasn't taught when the child was fifteen, it was taught at a very young age by its mother and other members of the community who were sharing in the child's upbringing. Same as today.

During the early millennia, survival depended on two main elements: food and shelter. Clothing and children were important but one could survive, for a while anyhow, without them but without food and shelter you'd be toast for sure.

As instincts faded out and a rudimentary language began to emerge, Homo sapiens developed an intuitive understanding of the importance of children.

Instinct is different than intuition.

Instinct is behavior that is unlearned and as such is unknown to the individual. Instinctual behavior is passed from generation to generation in almost identical fashion and the behavior is manifested identically among all individuals of the same species. Some instincts may be gender specific, which means that females of a species may behave differently than the males but all the females of that species behave in the same fashion and the same applies to the males.

By contrast, intuition is learned and is not passed from generation to generation and is not manifested identically among all individuals of the same species. Intuition is the act of knowing or sensing without reasoning. It is immediate cognition generated through experience.

We call it a *feeling*.

Some actions or situations *feel* right and others don't – intuition.

Intuitively then, Homo sapiens figured out that the investment of time and food for the child would reap benefits in terms of making the community grow and thereby increase its possibility of success in a very hostile world.

As a result, a little more liberal view on physical "correctness" began to develop. Those communities that were lucky enough to have an adequate food supply were able to support, probably at the mother's insistence, those individuals that didn't or couldn't directly contribute to the gathering of food and those individuals had some free time.

Free time = thinking = innovation = increased probability of survival.

Total specialization was not a high priority because death and disaster were common occurrences. You couldn't afford to have one person specialize in tool making because that person would probably die soon, cut his/her hand on some shale or just fall and break a leg. Suddenly the group was left with no tools. Everybody, male and female, had to do a little of everything.

Because communication skills and reasoning weren't very well refined, it was important for each clan to be as homogeneous as possible so you could take care of business without having to look over your shoulder at your neighbor because you thought he/she might be a little weird.

The birth of prejudice.

The rejected individuals went off to form clans of their own.

Some of those rejected didn't go too far and became competitors for territory and food.

This competition thing was the beginning of the invention of the rule.

As I mentioned, everyone had to be able to perform all the jobs to allow the clan to survive, but women had the extra job of birthing. Depending on the woman and the offspring, that job could suck up a lot of time and resources. After a couple of raids by the rejects, the people figured out that not all women were always available for defense but many women were.

As a result, a new job was created: protecting and raiding.

Naturally, strength and a specific kind of cunning became prized traits for this job and young people were trained in those skills. If a young man or woman became masterful at the necessary skills, she or he was admired, respected and feared.

Literature and folklore all over the world abounds with tales of women warriors. Here's a short list: Vishpala (pre India), Sammurmat (Assyria), Zenobia (Palmyrene which is now Syria), Mulan (now a cartoon hero but actually a real warrior), Tomde Gozan (Japanese Samurai) Deborah (Israel), the Amazons (Greek), Hatshesut (Egypt), Judith (Israel) and Joan of Arc.

About fifteen minutes of research will reveal many more and those you find are only the famous ones. There were thousands of others that were foot soldiers, Lieutenants, Captains and Generals but we still choose to believe that women should not be combatants, history and current situations to the contrary.

Anyhow, back to the fledgling Homo sapiens trying to survive.

There is a popular perception that the folks at this time were big tough guys running around in animal skins, spears in hand, hunting down Mastodons.

Not true.

We got that idea from cave drawings made by hominids (probably females) that are no longer with us. The survivors (us) were small, probably around four and a half feet tall and forty to sixty pounds in weight. They were terrified of almost everything and rightfully so. They huddled together in groups for protection from a very hostile world filled with storms, drought, cold, heat, and all sorts of creepy crawly things big and small. They did everything in groups. They hunted in packs like the other predators and probably scavenged a lot like the hyena. They ate a lot of fruit, legumes, tubers and bugs that they found growing about. Hunting down a Mastodon or a big buffalo was the last thing anybody wanted to do.

Eventually, over thousands of years, some people figured out the tools and tactics required to hunt the big boys but initially staying alive is what they wanted and communication, teamwork and cunning was the ticket.

Some communities like the Neanderthal didn't get it and perished. The Neanderthal had the brain capacity but they were barrel-chested, muscular guys and required a lot of protein to survive, other smaller hominids, not so much. As a result of their size and requirement for a lot of protein rich food, their communities never got very large (probably no more than 30 individuals) and they apparently didn't understand gender parity. Males did most of the hunting and women were not held in high esteem. Poor distribution of labor. As a result they perished ether from lack of food or the smaller, cleverer hominids kicked their butts or bred with them or all of the above.

There you have it. Women and men were equal members of a team whose objective was to survive. Both genders had pretty much the same jobs except women had one more job than the men and while a woman was doing her unique job, other members of the community, male and female, had to take up the slack. Logic dictates that once a child was weaned or another mother was lactating (nursemaids), the mother went back to her other duties and left the toddler in the care of other, probably older, women and/or men.

If all of this seems to be similar to the way we operate today, it's because it is. The physiological differences in terms of brain capacity and operation are not significantly deferent from the Hominids of 10 to 15 thousand years ago. We just have a whole lot more data.

There are still some clowns harping that women are smaller, weaker and have a propensity for "domestic" work.

Baloney, I say.

That narrow view is has no basis on fact. Strength was important, but only for some jobs. Cunning and teamwork was the key to survival as the last Neanderthal discovered as he/she expired. Some females, then as now, were stronger than some males; some males, then as now, excelled at things domestic and some females, then as now, were more cunning than some males.

Parity in terms of status and distribution of labor between males and female was essential for survival.

That is only part of the story.

The other part is control of the womb.

In the old days, 7 million years ago, females controlled their wombs.

Just like their animal ancestors, they must have had cycles when they were in "heat" and then and only then was she able to conceive. There have been some biological changes over the years, but women can still only breed when they are ovulating. When that ovulating period occurs is not as pronounced as it was nor is it as regular, but if she doesn't drop an egg, nothing happens and a good time is had by all.

Males want to breed all the time so it was up to the female to whack him on the head and stop him from fooling around.

A prehistoric "I've got a headache".

Nowadays the man should whack himself in the head and stop fooling around without protection.

Most of the Igors of the time, just like now, put up with this kind of behavior because if they made an unwanted move, he'd get whacked or today he'd be charged with sexual harassment or spousal abuse.

I think the old cartoon, which depicts the caveman dragging a female into the cave by the hair, is backwards. I think it was the female who was doing the conking and dragging because she and only she decided when it was time to breed, or have fun or both.

We still *ask* for her hand in marriage.

Females of a lot of species do the mate selecting. The guys run around butting heads or whatever to gain her attention and in the final analysis, she chooses. Based on her perception of important traits, certain males were selected for breeding and others were discarded.

Selective breeding determined by the female.

If the female either had no vote or chose unwisely then the species would perpetuate traits that were not the best for survival.

Just ask all the hominids that are no longer with us.

A similar comparison of how this works can be made with dogs.

Dogs and wolves are genetically very close (some say indistinguishable) but dogs have very different behavior patterns.

If a group of people lived in some sort of a community, there had to be trash. You know discarded carcasses, used up skin hides, that sort of thing. The people probably had some sort of a trash dump away from where they were living. The trash would attract wolves to get some treats.

When a person would approach to dump something, most of the wolves would scamper away, but some didn't go as far as others. That is called a short flight distance. Since the people didn't want to mess with the wolves, the two animals would be wary of one another. Some wolves and some people (probably a female – remember the bonding thing in the brain) overcame their trepidation and soon some of the wolves wouldn't flee at all perhaps even following the person to their cave or hut.

It wouldn't be too long before the short flight wolves would hang around and expect to be fed. Little wolves came along and some portion of the litter exhibited tameness and the people let them survive while the others became stew. Four or five generations of this selective breeding (four or five years) and you have a dog. Dogs then became an integral part of the community and began to help with the hunt, protection and general amusement – who doesn't love a puppy?

The same thing happened with other animals like goats, sheep, yaks, etc. depending on where the people lived. From that came a steady supply of protein, material for clothes and tools, milk and eventually cheese. All as a result of selective breeding.

People are the same way. As long as the female had a vote in the mate selection process, the species thrived and because no two women are alike and they have no instincts, variety began to appear.

Races.

Dog breeds.

Hmmm.

Love a puppy, a very casual remark but of incredible importance to the development of the techniques required for us to survive.

Nobody woke up one morning and decided that loving a puppy was reasonable behavior. To get to the point that people could actually conceive of domesticating another animal species, which involves care and feeding of something not part of the clan, required that certain complex emotions be in place and accepted.

Other species don't have complex emotions; it may seem like they do but they don't.

If that is true and we evolved from animals, how did we acquire emotions?

Remember that I mentioned the speech thing and that some offspring that were not as "correct" as others were allowed to survive? If a mother should insist, probably violently, that one of her offspring should not be harmed, she was developing abstract emotions that had very little to do with the survival of the entire group.

The same thing applied when some woman brought home a wolf or a yak.

The separation of people from animals was beginning and the impetus for that separation was driven by the females through her development of those "female" characteristics that that we call emotional like love, compassion, empathy, etc. Behavior that was radically different than her animal ancestors. Naturally, she intuitively passed on that information to each of her offspring and the painfully slow process of civilizing began.

Without the female's connection to the process of life and her emotional rather than rational attachment to another human, we would still be living in caves, if at all.

Thus emotions, developed, transmitted and nurtured by women are one of the essential characteristics of our species and became, in time, a primary tool for our survival, which is demonstrated in the domestication of animals.

It is not too large a leap to assume that the female's need to express her emotions is the foundation for developing language and eventually writing.

Somewhere along the line she lost control, probably ten to fifteen thousand years ago.

Here is my view of what happened.

Socially, the group thing was the preferred method of living. The concept of parenthood or "marriage" had not been established. As a matter of fact, tribes in New Zeeland, the Philippines, South America and Africa still live that way and the task of child rearing is shared as well as the indiscriminate sexual favors of both genders.

Because food is plentiful, space is confining, travel is difficult, the equatorial weather is relatively benign and shelter is relatively easy to acquire, the jungle folks pretty much stagnated. In the forests and plains of Europe, the Middle East, Mongolia and Southern China, movement was essential because good shelter was hard to find, the weather is more erratic and the sources of food were constantly disappearing or relocating.

Eventually, probably by chance, some clans figured out how to make lasting shelters and were able to stay in one place for long periods of time. Other groups began carrying their shelter with them. The settlers eventually became civilizations, but it would take many millennia for the Huns, the Visigoths, the Mongols and groups of that stripe to figure out that settling in one place is more cost effective and efficient. Maybe some people were just dumber than others or maybe it was just the climate. Living on the Steppes where its cold most of the time and food is hard to find is bound to piss you off some, while life can be pretty sweet living by the Nile, Tigris, Euphrates or Yangtze.

Not everyone stayed in one place.

Remember the selective breading thing and the slightly different genetic makeup of each individual in our species?

Some people were born with blue eyes and paler skin. Some women thought that was hot and bred with those men. Pretty soon, less than one hundred years, you've got a little clan of whities. To them the desert sun wasn't so cool and probably the rest of the clan who were "normal" didn't like it either. In either case the whities moved on. Five miles a day, three hundred days, equals fifteen hundred miles – a long way but not too long a time.

Baghdad to Berlin, 2000 miles.

The people were spreading out all over the planet.

There were two issues with wandering about. One was that the people were constantly challenged with new, often incomprehensible data like geography, weather, vegetation and animals. Good exercise for the brain matter, tough on survival. The other issue was that tribal knowledge got lost in the transition. The old were constantly being left behind. Nobody could write so everything learned by the clan resided in the heads of the older folks and when you left them behind because you had to move, a lot of information was lost.

"Come on Moms, we've got to move on."

"Why?"

"'Cause we've always moved on."

"Why?"

Igor thought for a little while.

"Don' no."

Moms continued: "We've got plenty of game, we've got trees and mud to make houses, some of the girls got stuff growing that we can eat and George figured out how to get fish from the river. What the hell do you want to move for?"

"No reason, I guess."

"Good, we're staying! I want a house with a view of the river and I want to tell you how to predict storms."

"OK"

Settling down in one place brought about all kinds of changes but, in this context, the most significant change was the male/female relationship.

As I said before, people skills and relationships weren't very high on the priority list when the main focus was bringing home the bacon and making it through the day without getting eaten, mauled or conked on the head. Now that people started to reside in one place, food and shelter were reasonably well under control and babies were not dying like flies certain men and certain women would form little subcultures within the clan and develop loyalties to each other in terms of food gathering and child rearing thereby forming families.

Labor division within the new family was/is a little more difficult because when the woman was birthing and caring for the infant(s) there was no one to take up the slack except for the one man.

Why this started to happen is not clear to anyone. Surely the communal thing was more efficient, the division of labor more effective and the old people had real jobs, so why change?

Nobody knows.

My theory is that when folks emerged from caves or stopped wandering in the savannahs they probably built large communal huts like the tribes I mentioned before. Life was pretty good and the population started to increase which required that the shelter space be increased. Decisions had to be made as to who was moving to the new hut and who was staying.

Right about then, some comely lass, about three months pregnant, snuggled up to George and suggested that they move to a smaller shelter with a couple of old folks and her two other children. Poor George, a little worn out from boinking her, acquiesced and a family was born. George and Lisa built their own hut and moved in.

That old black magic has me in its spell
That old black magic that you weave so well…
You are the lover that I've waited for
The mate that fate had me created for
And every time your lips meet mine
Baby down and down I go,
all around I go
In a spin, loving the spin that I'm in
Under that old black magic called love

Don't like that scenario? Maybe Eve and the apple suit your tastes better. Or aliens. Or that Intelligent Design dude.

For whatever reason, the behavior changed from communal to a more or less monogamous approach and right about then things started to go south for women in terms of parity and control.

Here's the problem. Let's say the woman is reasonably fertile and she gives birth to five children and three live. Now that the whole community isn't sharing her workload, she is essentially out of the food gathering and tribal defending business for at least six years or possibly nine years depending on the spacing of the children. If she gave birth to her first at fourteen, she would be out of business until about twenty-three, well into middle age considering that most people only lived about forty years.

See, the whole quasi-monogamy thing didn't make much sense from a pure survival point of view, but in their new digs along the river, life was not nearly as harsh, crops were coming in, kids were playing, the sun was shining, people were not being offed just because they didn't contribute as much and survival was not the pressing thing it used to be in the good old days.

Anyhow, George and Lisa set up shop and most everyone else thought the idea was a good one and they followed suit. George suddenly became the family provider. That was probably OK for old George but not so OK for old Lisa.

Communal (sharing) living pretty much disappeared from the scene and the concept of property emerged.

"Those are MY melons and if I see your kids snitching some again, I'll kick your ass!"

Property, an important concept.

Here's the deal, property was conceptualized before person. What that means is that people had a pretty good idea of property ownership but didn't have a real good idea of personal worth. People viewed each other as property rather than persons. The *idea* of "person" as opposed to a thing or an animal wouldn't gain universal acceptance until thousands of years later and in many cases we still have trouble with that concept.

You *belong* to me.

(Songs by Carly Simon, Vonda Shepard, Anita Baker, etc.)

There was no reason for them to think otherwise. The people had lived in close proximity to nature and for thousands of years. They learned how to survive from other animals and thought of themselves as another animal. The idea that a person had intrinsic worth in and of her/himself was completely foreign. Sure people had affection for one another, but in the final analysis people were property.

Here's how that came to be. Remember that some members of the clan were allowed to live that didn't directly contribute to the food gathering business? Somebody had to feed them.

You feed your dog -- it belongs to you.

You feed your woman -- she belongs to you.

Same deal.

The provider became the owner.

Conflicts within the community began to arise over ownership of things and people. Not that conflicts didn't happen before, but now there were a lot more people, possibly a couple of hundred, which meant a geometric increase in conflicts.

Rules had to be made and to have rules you've got to have a Ruler, an arbitrator if you will. Of course, the ruler liked the arrangement of being the boss and she/he and his/her buddies made up all sorts of rules to perpetrate his/her power.

Religion?

I digress.

Anyhow, a ruler was chosen. How a Ruler was chosen is not material, but chosen he/she was and rules of social behavior were established.

Then as now, most people went along with the rules and a semblance of order was established in the community.

Most rules dealt with property issues and almost everyone was someone's property. The Ruler, head of the clan or tribal leader owned almost everyone. Children were the property of their mothers and fathers and as such they were traded for cash or the equivalent.

A spear maker needed a helper to learn the trade. His neighbor had a young boy who looked promising. Money or goods were exchanged and the boy was now the spear maker's property (apprentice). Girls were handled the same way and "sold" as workers and brides. Whole families, men included, were indentured to someone else.

Rules were established to cover the transaction.

Some rules were a little vague.

Marital relationships for example.

Every now and then, one member of a family, male or female, would try to get a little boinking on the side for pleasure. Extramarital activity, then and now caused some confusion and probably violence, which disrupted the whole community. You couldn't have men fighting men, women fighting women or women fighting men over who was boinking whom.

Bad for the food gathering business.

Igor, the current Ruler, called a meeting.

"This is lion shit!" He declared.

The crowd gasped.

"What the hell is going on here?"

There was a murmur.

"George whacked Andrew in the head and he will be out of commission for a while and then Lisa stabbed George and he's dead. Betty is pissed and insists on taking care of Andrew. Now I got two of my best hunters, Betty and Andrew, out and the hunt starts next week. Somebody's going hungry and it ain't gonna be me and Elvira and my five rug rats."

He had their attention.

"We gotta make some rules."

The crowd nodded in understanding.

"What are we going to do about this boinking out of the family, business?"

There was a lot of fidgeting and lowering of eyes because, then as now, a lot of people were fooling around.

Nobody wanted to suggest anything.

Igor, being a politician, didn't like the idea of making up the rules himself (he was seeing Esmeralda) so he did what every wise politician does so he wouldn't get stuck with any fallout and he could claim plausible deniability. He set up a committee to investigate.

"Really?" You ask.

I have no idea, but it's obvious that something was going on because all sorts of rules have been found delineating "correct" behavior in this area and at some time somebody had to have had a similar conversation or else they wouldn't have written them down.

The Ten Commandments may have been a possible exception.

Hold that thought.

OK, where are we? The folks have been out of the caves for a few thousand years, villages have sprung up, communication skills were improving rapidly, Gates 1st was fiddling around with time and binary code – just kidding, writing – folks were getting some measure of control over their lives and they had Rulers and committees.

"What do you mean by committees?" You may ask.

Back in the good old days, the people were pretty much at a loss to understand what was happening around them. The seasons, the weather, the sun, the moon, disease and even the cause of birth perplexed and frightened them. They didn't understand anything and pretty much went with the flow of things. At some time, they started to ask: "What's up with that?"

One small question for an individual, one giant step for the people.

Coupled with asking why, was the idea of what are we going to do about it.

People were becoming people instead of animals.

Those questions bounced around for a few thousand years and probably were the impetus for people to leave the caves and set up villages.

Remember the old people? Those folks over thirty? They had seen the clouds forming and heard the distant rumbling of thunder and could predict with some degree of certainty that a storm was coming. They had seen the seeds spit on the ground and plants come out of the ground where the seeds had fallen.

The 0 to 15 crowd? Then as now, they had other pursuits.

Anyhow, some of the old folks, mostly women (life expectancy, remember) could see that the people were frightened when the storm clouds were forming and did little things to calm them down. For instance, she could remember the signs of a distant storm heading in their direction and the signs of a distant storm that would pass them by. So, if she saw that a storm was going to pass them by, she would perform some little ritual and take credit for nature's actions and calm everybody down.

Religion.

All kinds of weird stuff was invented to explain what the people couldn't understand and those explanations had the added benefit of adding status (power) to whatever old person had the best success rate in the prediction business.

As they say, power corrupts, and absolute power corrupts absolutely and these old crones, female and male, rapidly became the power behind the throne of the Ruler – the committees. They set the rules, they defined the gods – the scarier and weirder the better – and they became the arbiters of social customs.

Mere human laws didn't seem to cut it so the committees decreed that god, which one is immaterial, had decided that the relationship among men and women had to follow certain patterns. Fear was instituted to keep the woman near the hearth and the man as the provider. Fear of the wrath of god and ostracism had better success at maintaining the social "order" than just passing a law.

Did you hold that thought?

The Ten Commandments.

One thing was becoming obvious with the new quasi-monogamous family arrangement was that if the woman should leave the unit by death or some other circumstance; the community had to pick up the slack in terms of caring for the children. Death was unfortunate and outside of the ability of human solution, but other circumstances could be avoided.

Another problem was the situation where the woman was barren. Since breeding was still of paramount importance, it was all right for the guy to acquire concubines for breeding purposes.

Says so in the Bible.

I told you that things were going bad for women once the communal system disappeared.

Seems pretty reasonable except for one little hitch. Men died more frequently or went off exploring or to war or whatever and the family was left provider-less. Big problem and different groups tried different methods to resolve this issue with varying degrees of success but in the final analysis, the woman had to get another provider or starve.

Generally she went back to her father or in some societies, she could cohabitate. When the old man returned from the wars or from the long business trip on a caravan, she had to come back, but any new children stayed with their father.

"What about men just abandoning their families for some hussy?"

Also not good and the penalties were harsh but in most societies a sort of alimony arrangement was established so the community didn't have to foot the bill to maintain the abandoned family. Cash, then as now, was king.

For the majority of people with no cash, the abandoned woman had brothers, uncles, fathers, sisters, daughters and sons who would hunt down the son of a bitch and kill him like a dog in the streets. Still happens.

If you want to read all the details, Hammurabi had his committee write down all the rules and his Code sort of became the standard in the Western world.

In summary then, women played an important role in the social fabric, were a source of power and had a more or less equal footing with everyone. Slowly, over the centuries, communal living (sharing) disappeared and the concept of property became paramount. Those that provided, e.g.: rulers, landowners, merchants, etc., owned things including people. Husbands owned wives because he had "bought" her from her father and provided for her and both of them owned their children, who, in turn, were traded for wealth.

Women lost parity and control of her womb.

Conking the old man on the head when he wanted to fool around was no longer acceptable.

The process of subdividing behavior characteristics began and the rule was invented.

There you have it, customs and usages of the social group came to be regarded as essential to its survival and welfare and became, through general observance, part of a formalized legal code.

Mores.

The status of a woman had nothing whatever to do with men being better, worse, dominant or any other sexist propaganda. The status of everyone is determined by the ideas, the mores, which have evolved over many centuries and have been codified into religious dogma, which eventually became secular law. The problem is not the people; rather the ideas that creep into our heads and make us *think* that we *must* behave in a certain way.

The behavioral traits now classified as female such as sensitivity to others, communicative, etc. were essential to the survival and social progress of the Homo sapiens and were a part of the accepted behavior of all members of the small clans.

As the clans grew in size and defensive or aggressive competition between clans began to emerge, characteristics such as aggression, competition, leadership, etc. began to be necessary for a particular clan to survive. The predators were no longer only other animals, they were also other people. By default, the job of defending the clan fell on men and those men who exhibited the proper characteristics were prized. Suddenly, boy children were prized and taught "maleness" and contributed to the family wealth while girl children had little or no value except as brides and were taught "woman's work" and the necessary techniques to become desirable. Sometimes girls were offered as an exchange for political or business alliances and dowries were developed to seal the contract. The custom of the father paying for his daughter's wedding comes from the dowry thing.

Because the leaders and the members of committees weren't too bright and worried about their survival, they immediately leapt to the conclusion that maleness was better than femaleness.

Apparently we haven't become any smarter.

Huge, and I mean HUGE error that has caused the species untold pain and is slowly inching us to our own demise.

Seven

Somebody Has to Clean Up this Mess!

As I said before, there was a huge public relations mistake that resulted in the elimination of parity for women and as a result they were edged out of all the committees except for very specific roles like oracles or vestal virgins. That left mostly men to invent, chronicle and interpret religious law. Naturally these old guys wanted to assure that there was plenty of progeny (get laid), so almost all the organized religions had/have dogmas, statements or rules about the position of women in society.

The primary religious belief that affected women, which became codified into civil law, was that she had to marry and breed.

She could be powerful, wealthy or even a queen but her primary role according to religious and civil law was to breed.

Contraception?

A no-no.

Men were allowed sexual "privileges", women had none.

Men could fool around, women were branded.

Does this sound familiar? "It is nature's way."

That concept is bizarre and perverted because it implies that women are only baby machines or life support systems for a womb.

Dehumanizing in the extreme.

Of course, the logical extension of that horrible concept is to "sanctify" marriage. I'm not a Biblical scholar but I couldn't find any commentary about marriage in the Bible except as tool for the acquisition of power or status. Daughters were married off at the direction of their fathers all over the place. Nowhere does it mention whether the girls were happy about the situation or not. The fact is, in the Western World, marriage was "sanctified" sometime about 800ACE (AD in the old days) by the reigning Christian Church of the time. Eventually it became a civil custom and law primarily for tax and control reasons.

Marriage is good and necessary if you decide to start a family, but that is only a small part of the picture. Marriage is about a shared bond which two people establish that involves respect, affection, mutual protection, shared goals, negotiation, anger, joy, memories, future and many other things. The marriage license legalizes and bestows cultural acceptance to that shared bond and establishes boundaries that limit the interference from the rest of society. The piece of paper also defines the two individuals as one entity, each responsible for the other and they, in turn, responsible for any offspring that may be forthcoming.

Important stuff marriage, but sacred…hardly.

When religions "sanctified" marriage they did it to assure the steady flow of "gifts from God" – children. At the same time they "sanctified" male dominance and abuse, you know, love honor and OBEY. A woman became the property of the man, which, as you can imagine, led to all kinds of nasty things happening to women. Things like the "Rule of Thumb" which decreed that the man could not beat his wife with a rod with a diameter larger than the width of his thumb.

Smaller than the old man's thumb? Whack her a good one!

Nowhere in this sanctity thing does it mention respect, affection, mutual protection, shared goals, negotiation, anger, joy, memories, future or any of other things that are a marriage.

Eventually governments, some of which have the good sense to separate church from state, decreed that abuse and male dominance is illegal.

That's why religions get their shorts in a bunch when people of the same gender want equal legal and social protection though marriage.

"Marriage is not to legitimize a bond between two people, it's for procreation." They screech.

Actually they don't say that, but that's what they mean.

They also mean that a man is dominant and a woman is merely a life support system for a womb.

The clan, class or species must be perpetuated.

Go forth and multiply.

To do that, all kinds of social rulings, mostly restrictive to women, were put in place to assure that successful breeding would occur. The more breeding the better and if the offspring are boys, better still. This baby-mill mentality was particularly prevalent among the poor who pretty much bred willy-nilly and that was OK because, well, they were poor and the rich needed the labor and the soldiers. Women with many children or multiple births were/are held in high regard. The fact that some women were/are literally fucked to death, mentally and physically, by too many children was/is ignored. Many wealthy women avoided that fate somehow, probably by primitive contraception and secret abortions. The poor? Nobody knows.

Of course the infant mortality rate was pretty high as well.

You don't suppose some children met an untimely death do you? A hand over the mouth while the baby slept?

Nah.

Not those fine Ladies of olden times.

Nah.

The poor? Nobody knows.

At some point in time, virginity became a big thing, primarily for the rich, not because it was moral or proper although that was the social mantra, but because it assured the purity of the bloodlines, class or heritage – like horses or something. If the virgin state was somehow violated, only the woman was/is held accountable.

How weird is that?

Even today, many people frown on "mixed" marriages. People of a particular class, social status, nationality or ethnic background are expected to marry and breed within their "class".

Archaic and stupid I say, but that's just me.

The whole concept of "protecting" women was and is a guise to assure that women were/are available to breed. Sports and other strenuous activities were discouraged lest the baby machine somehow become damaged.

Of course she could haul water from the well for three blocks and up a bunch of steps, or chop wood, or clean chandeliers at Versailles or harvest rice from a paddy or whatever. That was OK. That was woman's work.

That's the trouble with assuming someone else is inferior, there's a complete loss of reason.

We know now that sports or strenuous activity doesn't damage the machine, but there always seems to be some clown harping on the "lady-like" thing.

For a long time, even intellectual activity was discouraged; mainly because, god forbid, the damsel might discover that she doesn't have to put up with that lout of a husband assigned to her.

Can't win for losing. Hell, just staying even is tough enough.

As I mentioned before, because giving birth and its associated behavior is uniquely female and during the time that function is being performed, the female is more dependent and we leapt to the conclusion that "female" behaviors that are more pronounced during this period are dependent. Therefore, women are dependent and their activities are less important.

The people of Igor's time did not understand that those very traits of tenderness, warmth, compassion, affection, etc. which are the cornerstones of empathy and are the traits that allowed us to survive in the first place.

We still don't.

Because the people didn't understand they relegated women to fourth-class status (behind men, boy children and livestock) solely because the traits she exhibited during the breeding process were not conducive to defense or expansion of the clan.

If you think that it is difficult for us, modern, educated, etc. people to accept the possibility that people exhibit different behavioral traits at different times and in response to different situations, for the people of olden times it was impossible.

"People never change."

As a result, when women exhibited "male" traits she was weird.

As a result, when a man exhibited "female" traits he was weird.

Still that way.

The system of relegating women to fourth-class status worked pretty well in terms of increasing the population; in terms of everything else... the jury is still out.

Eventually we discovered sanitation and people stopped dying like flies.

Pretty soon there were a lot of people.

I decided to look at the world population situation and see what I could find.

I discovered that things are not good.

Look at this way, the population of the earth doubled from about 2.5 billion in 1950 to about 5.3 billion in 1990 and now stands at about 7.0 + billion and reproducing at the rate of one child born every four seconds. A lot of people and the majority live at just above subsistence level. It should be fairly obvious that at some point the planet cannot support any more folks.

Is that number eight billion? Is it 10 billion? Is it 100 billion? Nobody knows, but at some point it's too many and at that point "sanctity", status, wealth and all the trappings of civilization may take on whole other meanings.

Some people argue that the planet has plenty of space and that's true, but the problem isn't space, it's the availability of resources; you know, water, fuel and wealth. You can choose to ignore the fact that the amount of combustible fossil fuels is limited (not infinite) or the effect of all those people eating, drinking, shitting and otherwise moving about has on the planet, but at some point more energy is consumed faster than the planet can produce.

The planet is just a dumb machine, complicated but still dumb. It receives energy from the sun and its core, processes the energy to produce all the stuff all of the species (animal and vegetable) need to survive and leaves behind slag or unusable waste. If you ask the dumb machine to produce more energy than it receives, it can't and it breaks.

More people require more food, which requires more energy for plants and animals to supply that food, plus energy to distribute that food and energy to process more waste.

That's a lot of work for a dumb machine

The World Wildlife Fund (WWF) has some computer models that show that the population of the earth, human and otherwise, is using up energy at the rate of one planet's worth a year. Soon that use will be one planet's worth a day.

Accurate model? Who knows, but it is not out of the range of reason to predict that within the foreseeable future of the Baby Boomer's grandchildren, we will be using more energy than the planet can generate. When the effect of that starts to be felt, there will be savages at the gate of the wasteful industrialized world.

As a matter of fact, the current sentiment in the U.S. is to build a wall along the Mexican border to keep them out.

It won't work.

Of course one can always take the position that those things may happen "over there" but "over there" is only a few hours away by plane and a few seconds away by TV.

Not much different than the problems old Igor and his merry band had in the good old days.

Not enough food? Weed out the clan or move on or both.

Cave too full of crap? Weed out the clan or move on or both.

When the time comes that there are too many people on the planet and not enough resources, we will have to weed out the clan or move or both. Moving is pretty much out of the question so weeding will occur.

Millions, perhaps billions, of people will have to die in order that fewer of the species can survive on the remaining resources.

Not a pleasant prospect.

Apparently it's not accurate either because just the opposite seems to be occurring.

This little chart I borrowed from the Census Bureau shows what I'm talking about.

World Population Growth

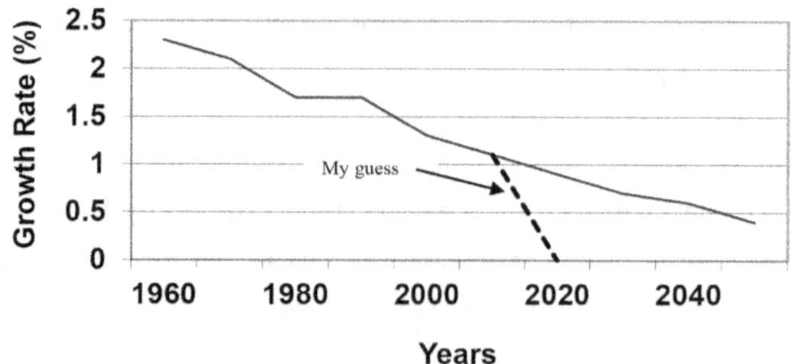

The chart shows that the *rate* of increase in the population of the world is decreasing. That is, the population is increasing at a slower rate than in the recent past and sometime around 2050 the rate will be zero.

I think it will happen sooner, but that's just me.

When the population growth reaches zero, the same number of people are dying as are being born and stability is achieved.

Calculating population growth is a fairly complicated problem, so let all the statisticians worry about the numbers. All I'm asking you to think about is that if the number of people being born equals the number of people dying, the population growth is zero. For that to happen 2+ children have to be born to each woman of childbearing age, two to replace each parent and the + is some number to account for accidents and natural disasters; generally people dying before their natural life expectancy of, say, 65.

That number most experts say is .1 and it equates to several million people each year. If you want the exact number you can figure it out on your own, but let me assure you that it's a lot of folks.

A little tangential thought here.

We are constantly hearing of all sorts of terrible natural disasters like hurricanes, tsunamis, earthquakes and pandemics and rightfully reel at the number of people involved. Somehow we feel that the world is not a very safe place and it makes us a little nervous.

Some people claim that these are messages from their God. An assumption that is not unlike the good old days when the high priests determined that the gods were angry and performed all sorts of rituals to appease them – sacrifice a thin virgin girl, for instance.

Take earthquakes and tsunamis. Those events have been occurring for a long time and will continue to occur far into the foreseeable future.

Are they more frequent?

I have no idea and I suspect that experts in the field don't know either.

Are they more frequent in recorded history?

Same answer.

For instance, in 1812 an earthquake occurred that traveled from Venezuela through the Gulf of Mexico. What the magnitude was I don't know but it made the Mississippi River flow upstream for several days. Had the population density along the river been what it is today with the crude construction standards of those days, hundreds of thousands if not millions of people would have been lost.

Nobody except Audubon and his cronies were there to record the event, so the loss of life was minimal and very few people even knew it occurred.

Today, with many people living in geologically high-risk areas, every time the Earth shrugs a little, a bunch of people die.

Besides we hear about it seconds after it happens. In the old days it would take months for anyone to find out if they found out at all.

The same issue occurs with hurricanes. Densely populated areas are in harm's way.

In 2005 we had a bunch of hurricanes in the Atlantic/Caribbean/Gulf of Mexico area. It's happened before and will no doubt happen again.

Global Warming?

Nobody knows.

Pandemics are the same deal. Too many people packed together in unhealthy conditions.

Incidentally, we used to call the outbreak of disease an epidemic but now, since an infected person can get on an airplane to wherever, it's a worldwide epidemic or pandemic.

If the worst case scenario unfolds for the Avian Flu or some other bug, 150 million will people die, which would be really bad, about 2.3% of the population.

Not good, but the plague that enveloped Europe in the Middle Ages killed off almost a third of the European population and we survived.

There is evidence to suggest that about 70,000 years ago there was a super volcano eruption called the Toba incident that reduced the human population to less than 2,000 breeding pairs and we barely survived.

What I'm trying to suggest with this little side issue is that disasters related to the normal operation of the planet have only a marginal effect on the total survivability of our species and the .1 number demographers use is to account for those incidents.

Anyhow, the rate of population growth is declining and declining sharply.

Here are some statistical facts. The fertility rate of the world dropped about 18% from 1990 to 2000 that means that several million less children were being born in 2000 than in 1990. For the less developed countries, the drop, about 34% (still more than 2.1), has been more dramatic while in the industrialized countries the rate has dropped 16% to about 1.6 children per female of child bearing age (14 to 45).

Are more people dying more frequently?

There seems to be no evidence of that.

If people aren't dying at a faster rate but the growth rate is decreasing, then it must be that fewer people are being born.

Why?

There is a small army of people working for the United Nations and other agencies trying to figure why the fertility rate is declining worldwide. In many places the rate has been below replacement levels (2.1 children) for decades. They make studies, have meetings and spend a lot of time scratching their heads because they have no reliable answers.

So what's going on?

Here's what I know:

1. There is a limit to the number of people that the planet can support. What that number is, nobody knows.

2. The fertility rate worldwide is dropping, i.e.: fewer children are being born per woman of childbearing age.

Question:

Is there a correlation between those two bits of information?

Only women give birth.

Fewer babies are being born…

Do a lot of women of childbearing age (14 to 45) have a *sense* that things are getting out of control?

Now there's an interesting hypothesis: women *sense* that there is an impending danger around the corner and manly men have no clue.

Is that a sexist hypothesis?

I have no idea, but it's intriguing.

I decided to run with this idea and see if it has any merit at all.

Before everyone gets excited, I do not mean all women nor do I exclude all men. Some women are insensitive and stupid and breed haphazardly with no concern for her clan, herself or the welfare of the new child. Conversely, some men are sensitive, caring, are very careful about impregnating a woman and should the event occur, those men take on the task of fathering with gusto and responsibility. Therefore when I speak of women in the context of child bearing, I am speaking about individuals, male or female, who embrace those "feminine" traits – affection, compassion, gentleness, sensitivity, sympathy, etc. – that are essential for child rearing and our survival.

To try and minimize any confusion, when I am speaking of men or women who embrace the traits I mentioned, I will use the word Wo/man in bold type.

Thus the sentence above should be read as follows: Now there's an interesting hypothesis: **Wo/man** *sense* that there is an impending danger around the corner and manly men or girly women have no clue.

Can it be possible that somehow **Wo/man** have a sense that we, as a species, are reaching the upper limit of sustainable population and are doing something about it?

Hmmm.

Even though I'm not too sure what *sense* means, I decided to investigate.

Obviously, proving or disproving an assumption like that cannot be done empirically, that is, lab experiments aren't going to work, so I'm going to have to use deduction; like Sherlock Holms.

One way to use deduction is to remove all the possibilities that don't make sense and then what's left is the conclusion.

Premises:

1. There is a limit to the number of people that the planet can support.
2. As we approach the limit, survivability becomes more difficult for many and many may be at risk of not surviving at all.
3. Since the 1960's the rate of population growth has been declining.

To be demonstrated:

1. **Wo/man** have a sense that we, as a species, are reaching the upper limit of sustainable population.
2. **Wo/man** are taking steps to avert the potential crisis of exceeding the sustainable population limit.

The first two premises are obvious in that eventually there will be too many people on the planet for all of us to survive and by survive I mean something other than sleeping in the streets or woods and rummaging through garbage cans for food and clothing.

That's already too prevalent a problem.

Obviously there will always be some number of people who will be destitute but it is reasonable to try and minimize that situation and thus improve or maintain the quality of life for most people.

Thus survival means to survive well, not just exist.

That utopian goal can only be achieved if there is some reasonable balance between the amount of available resources (water, land, animals, fish, etc.) and the number of people consuming them, which makes the first premise obvious. The population cannot increase indefinitely. Should that occur, nasty things like famine, disease, food riots, genocide, etc. will take place and threaten everybody.

Not good and obviously dangerous.

From the grid locked freeways of Los Angeles to the slums of Calcutta, people, men and women, everywhere know that there are too many of us. Some people try to move but pretty soon they find out that a bunch of other people have the same idea and soon the pristine area they have moved to is overpopulated.

Bummer.

Some places, China for instance, have recognized the danger of overpopulation and have instituted draconian measures to limit the birthrate. Other nations with population problems, as well as the United Nations, have launched massive information campaigns to try and limit population growth.

Much of the propaganda and concerted efforts by governments in various parts of the world to limit population is motivated by economics. If the population of some country or region is increasing rapidly, then resources that might be available to create jobs, infrastructure and wealth must be made available just to feed, clothe and shelter the population. This diversion of resources results in a perpetual cycle of poverty and civil unrest.

Haiti.

The obvious signs of this difficulty are famine, genocide, and corruption as a few people try to hoard what few resources are available.

The less obvious signs are malnutrition, economic stagnation and widespread poverty, conditions that exist in a significant portion of the planet.

You know, tourist destinations.

Further, because of globalization, we can no longer ignore catastrophes that happen in other parts of the world. In the good old days, the slaughter of over a million people in the killing fields of Cambodia or the slaughter of millions of Armenians met with a big ho-hum. Now, some birds get sick in a rural province in China that no one ever heard of and alarms go up all over the world.

OK, people all over are beginning to understand (have a sense) that continued population growth is, in the long run, life threatening for many and, because of the interdependence of the global economy, overpopulation may even be threatening to them personally or at least to that thing we call "life-style".

The third premise speaks to the declining rate of population growth.

One can easily leap to the conclusion that the reduction of the fertility rate is closely related to economics; meaning that people in wealthier regions of the world have the resources and education to better control their birth rate.

Not a bad assumption except that the fertility rate is dropping more rapidly in the less developed countries (except for the very poorest) than in the more developed countries. (*Ref. United Nations Department of Social and Economic Affairs, World Population Prospects, 2006 Revision. www. un.org/esa/population/unpop.htm*)

Why?

Experts from all over the world are trying to figure out why the rate is dropping and they have generally concluded that education, economics, wealth, religion and whatever else they can think of seem to have no consistent effect.

They just don't know what is happening.

Is there less boinking going on?

No evidence of that, just the opposite may be the case.

So, like old Sherlock, I have considered all of the possibilities and found them wanting.

"What's the answer?"

"Elementary, Dr. Watson. The only remaining possibility is that **Wo/man** know of the danger and are taking steps to save or at least protect the species."

There are several problems with this conclusion.

The first problem is that I am presuming that the worldwide drop in the fertility rate, which is caused by many women having fewer babies, relates directly to what an individual woman does or doesn't do.

I think it is fair to assume that not many women think of the world situation, much less the species, when they decide to procreate. She thinks of a lot of things or doesn't think at all but I don't think that a woman in Tulsa thinks of the impact her baby might have on the people of Punjab. If she thinks about it at all, she probably thinks of herself, her husband, father, mother, aunts and uncles, other children, friends, etc.; in short, her clan.

That is exactly how we all operate. When we decide to do or not to do something we take into consideration the effect our actions will have on our clan – worrying about the whole species is way too difficult.

My conclusion states that many, many **Wo/man** have decided that having fewer children is more beneficial (less danger) to themselves and their clan than having many children and since the aggregate of all the clans is the species, it follows that the decision to have fewer children in a clan affects the whole species.

Therefore, **Wo/man**, at the family or clan level, know of the danger of overpopulating their clan and are taking steps to save or at least protect their clan and the cumulative effect of those individual actions are projected on to the entire human population of the world – the species.

Another problem with the conclusion is similar to the chicken and the egg quandary: which came first the chicken or the egg?

Which came first: knowledge of the danger or the "steps"?

Which was it?

Did **Wo/man** have a knowledge that the species (clan) was in danger due to overpopulation and try and solve that problem

Or

Is the declining fertility rate an accidental consequence of political, scientific and social changes affecting women during the last 50+ years?

I suspect that the demographers and other members of the scientific community would prefer to assume that the declining fertility rate is an unintended consequence of sociological changes. That assumption supports the rule, i.e.: women either singularly or collectively could not possibly cause changes in social behavior on their own.

Bullshit and sexist to the extreme!

Since I don't support the rule, I say that a large motivator in the sociological changes over the last century has been a concerted effort by **Wo/man** to stop being barefoot and pregnant.

I spent a great deal of time observing *superficial* behavior that is performed because of the rule, but make no mistake, that superficial behavior does not necessarily translate into triviality in all things.

A substantial number of **Wo/man** know now and have known for some time that there is more to life than just popping out babies and know now and have known for some time that too many babies is not a good thing; not for them and not for the clan. As a result, the real unintended consequence of **Wo/man** search to find a solution to the baby thing has resulted in a substantial improvement in the quality of their lives and the quality of the life of the clan. Not the other way around.

Therefore, the reduction in the fertility rate is an <u>intentional</u> result of **Wo/man** searching for ways to improve the life of the clan or at least reduce the danger and the sociological changes are the consequence.

It's my theory and I'm sticking to it: **Wo/man** know of the danger and are taking steps to save or at least protect the species.

Which brings up the question of what "know" means and what "steps" am I talking about.

Let's eat the elephant one bite at a time.

Know.

We all understand what "to know" means.

Philosophers and scientists have been beating their heads against a brick wall for centuries to try and define how and what we know; all they got was a headache.

I don't buy into that.

I take the simple approach.

Everybody understands that there are different levels of knowing.

Just for the hell of it, let's number the levels even though the levels may overlap some and we may operate on different levels at the same time.

For instance, you know that the sun comes up in the morning. You also know that the sun doesn't really "come up" but that the Earth rotates. You don't care because worrying about those technicalities makes life and communication way too difficult.

So when you read in the paper that "sunrise" is at 6:27AM, you accept that and move on.

OK, that's level one of knowing: facts, data, figures of speech and stuff like that which gets us through the day.

We could care less if the information is technically correct or even accurate. If you get paid on Friday, it's good enough.

The words we use at this level are primarily nouns like tree, car, house, etc., very few adjectives or verbs.

The second level of knowing is stuff like mathematics or arithmetic.

We know that 6+8 = 14. We don't know why exactly, but it doesn't matter. It's a convention that we use to navigate through our checkbook so we can know if we have enough money to buy that neat little gizmo.

At the same level we know about time, distance, weight, etc., stuff that allows us to navigate through the world. Again accuracy is not essential but it is helpful. Keeps the bank from charging us an over-draft fee.

Here's where we use some adverbs and simple adjectives like about, tall, short, green, etc.

At the third level, some of the things we know become a teeny bit shaky.

For instance we, some better than others, know about cause and effect. You drop a glass and you know it's going to break. Sometimes it doesn't – you were lucky. See, a little bit shaky because a certain cause doesn't always bring about the expected result.

At this level we also know about things like the car starting in the morning, black clouds bring rain, no studying causes bad grades, etc.

Probability things learned through experience.

This is the level that we use words like probably, maybe, I think so, etc., verbs and adverbs

At the fourth level we take things on faith with very little actual proof and know them.

One can say that I know my wife loves me and I love her, there is a God, there isn't a God, Capitalism is good, etc. Very shaky ground, but all of us operate on faith "knowledge" as if it were reality and we use words that have vague definitions or multiple definitions like faith, feel, appears, etc.

Sometimes we get in trouble.

This level of knowing is what causes most of the confusion among humans.

This level of knowing is the level at which we establish many of our priorities.

In that way, **Wo/man** know things that manly men and girly women don't.

Manly men, for the most part, know about overpopulation in the same way that one knows about physical or mathematical problem. X amount of people consume a Y amount of resources; if X becomes larger than Y…

You know what I mean. Manly men approach overpopulation as a problem to be solved. They pass laws start advertising campaigns or whatever.

Manly men view the problem at the third level of knowing with a tiny, tiny bit of the fourth level thrown in.

Girly women just don't give a shit.

Wo/man, on the other hand, know about the problem at the fourth level.

Weird.

Actually not so weird because we are talking about population which means people which means life.

Most men and many women don't understand life at the same level as **Wo/man.** Sure they know about it and respect it, but we don't have a real sense of it. They don't have the same connection as **Wo/man.**

Most **Wo/man** are more in tune with vitality than manly men and most **Wo/man** are females.

vi·tal·l·ity *n.* That which distinguishes the living from the nonliving: an energy, force or principal characteristic of life.

Female **Wo/man** are more in tune. They understand that the menstrual cycle always brings with it the potential for new life, while menopause…? They are the first to feel a new life and only they can truly experience the joy, fear, hope, despair, panic, elation and sense of awe that the first stirrings of a new life growing within her brings.

Not to mention pickles and chocolate ice cream.

If we can agree that most **Wo/man** have a visceral or personal connection with vitality then it stands to reason that they *know*.

What's really weird is that this *knowing* extends beyond the immediacy of family; it extends universally. That is, **Wo/man** in Bangladesh, for instance, have the same *knowledge* as **Wo/man** in Cairo.

In that way, human **Wo/man** are connected with each other through their knowledge that a human life is not an abstract concept, it is a reality, it is palpable, it has value and as such it must be protected.

Given all of that, one would assume that maximizing the amount of life is a good thing.

Unfortunately, that's the male approach: beer is good therefore more beer is better.

Or, as in the good old days: A good wife produces many children, preferably male children

Wo/man are saying: "Not necessarily."

No mother wants to be in the situation wherein she has produced more life than she can nurture and that seems to be one of the common threads that unite **Wo/man** in their knowledge.

Just a question here to piss you off: Are women and men who use artificial means of procreating instead of adopting just breeders?

I know someone is pissed off about that question.

Anyhow, **Wo/man** know now and have known for some time that there is more to survival than just producing life. The life produced must survive and survive well.

You know, be happy, successful or whatever.

Just existing at some level barely above starvation isn't going to cut it and **Wo/man** in Wichita, New Delhi, Brisbane or wherever empathize with each other and know that too many members of the clan diminishes the quality of life and have decided to do something about it.

You may think that conclusion is a bit much but, like I said before, eventually the number of us will outstrip the available resources and if the birth rate doesn't decrease the death rate will have to increase in order for the remaining humans to survive with fewer resources, and if that happens the world may begin to look like Uganda.

The few "haves" will hoard and the "have-nots" will starve.

Wo/man collectively are saying: "Hmmm…I don't think so."

Fewer babies.

I'm reasonably certain that the demographers don't accept the possibility that **Wo/man** are somehow connected and have collectively decided to reduce the number of babies being born.

That would be unscientific and impossible to prove.

Absolutely true, but we are talking about **Wo/man** and babies and love and fear and lust and rejection here, topics that don't lend themselves to scientific inquiry.

Or you may say: "That's a bunch of hooey!"

"There are a lot of reasons for the population growth to be slowing. Education is probably the most significant." You may persist.

Education?

What kind of education?

School? Sex Education?

What?

Only partially correct.

I don't mean to put down the women conferences and the propaganda issued by various governments, because they are a source of information, education if you will, but the fact is that a person has to *feel* a certain way for the information to take hold.

Not a very precise word, feel, but if you want precision talk about machines not people.

Besides, giving birth is far, far too personal, too visceral, too intuitive and too hormonal to be controlled by just imparting information. You must change the way people *feel* about the process before you can get them to learn.

Change the hearts and minds.

Wo/man worldwide are beginning to *feel* differently about big families than they did in the recent past.

You may like to believe that education teaches about population control, but the truth is that education only supplies the techniques, like contraception, not the desire.

You can't educate someone if they don't want to listen, but **Wo/man** worldwide want to listen and they are putting into practice what they hear.

Not only are they listening but they know and are *intuitively* passing on the message that there are too many of us (their clan) to survive well. Education and science are finally providing the tools to make the implementation of that knowledge a reality.

in·tu·i·tion *n.* The act or faculty of knowing without the use of rational process; immediate cognition.

Mothers, in their process of communicating with the very young, have started to change the accepted traditional customs and usages of their particular social group and are imparting new customs that they regard as essential to our survival and welfare.

Wo/man worldwide are changing the mores of their cultures from the more the merrier to less is better.

How they do that, no one knows for sure.

The reduction in population growth is just the result of the sense that **Wo/man** have that the species (their clan) is in danger of not surviving well.

They know the answer to the problem (too many people in the clan) and are taking steps to solve it.

Because of their intimacy with the process, **Wo/man** *know* about life, about survival, about protection and about danger more acutely that the rest of the species.

Many **Wo/man** are intuitive about these things and can "smell" the danger to the survival of the species (their clan).

Their immediate cognition tells them of the danger and motivates them to do something about it and nobody can stop them.

Nor should we want to.

Male Moguls haven't got a clue.

Hell, many governments can't even accept the *possibility* that there may be too much pollution stemming from too many people burning too much stuff.

Most men, on the other hand, follow their woman's lead because they are caring, responsible and mature.

Most men have solid relationships with women and value her opinions on everything from politics to the family budget.

Most men realize that when it comes to raising children, she makes most of the decisions and like most of the "what to wear" decisions, he stays out of the way.

That's why the burly football play says "Hi Mom" from the sidelines, not "Hi Dad".

Lastly, most men realize that contraception, male or female, means more boinking, not less.

Good deal.

Therefore, since most women and men operate as a team in this regard, cultures worldwide are accepting the **Wo/man's** stand that less is better and the mores are evolving.

Some cultures more rapidly than others.

Yeah, yeah, I'm oversimplifying complex sociological forces that are at work.

Am I?

You decide.

Me, I'm a simple kind of a guy.

Talk about complex sociological forces only disguises reality.

You may scream, yell and jump up and down and come up with all kinds of logical "reasons" explaining why the fertility rate is dropping.

"Women are breaking the oppressive shackles of the past and realize that they are not defined by husband and family"

Yup. Not a life support system for a womb.

"Large families are not economically viable."

Yup. Not enough resources.

"The world is too dangerous a place"

Yup. Too many folks.

"Women are delaying or abstaining from giving birth because they are selfish and want it all"

That's too stupid to even comment on.

Etc., etc.

Me, I'm a simple guy and I'll say it again: **Wo/man** *feel* differently than they did in the past about large families and that *feeling* is the result of **Wo/man** having an *intuitive* understanding of the danger facing the species (their clan) due to overpopulation.

All women?

All men?

Of course not, but enough **Wo/man** to make a difference.

All it takes is for 60% of the women to decide to have two or less children and about 15% of the women to choose to have no children and the fertility rate is below 2.1.

Look deep down inside yourself and think about how you feel when you see a woman with four or five children under the age of ten.

Admiration or pity?

Envy or disdain?

Since the fertility rate in the United States has been hovering around 1.8 to 2.0 for the last several decades, I can only assume that having five children is not high on the list of priorities.

"Maybe it's an instinct thing." You may surmise.

Nope.

Instinct is different than intuition.

Instinct is behavior that is unlearned and as such is unknown to the individual.

Intuition is learned and is not passed from generation to generation and is not manifested identically among all individuals of the same species.

For instance, a person may learn from her/his mother and/or father the basic rules of behavior but can, as he/she matures chose to accept or reject some or all of the rules. This rejection/acceptance process may or may not be conscious. That is, the individual may not necessarily understand or be able to concisely verbalize the why of the acceptance or rejection of a particular rule or set of rules.

It just doesn't *feel* right.

Because some behavior doesn't *feel* right, the individual will tend to surround himself/herself with other people of similar values, reject information that is contrary to the new *feelings* and accept information that supports the new attitudes. We humans, in general, chose our mates based on those feelings.

Since this whole process of learning the behavioral rules and then rejecting or accepting them is more subliminal than logical, it is intuitive.

Instinctual behavioral rules, on the other hand, cannot be rejected by the next generation.

Ducks don't get a vote on what they want to do; they just migrate to wherever it is that they migrate.

They don't even avoid hunters, year after year.

Peking Duck, anyone?

Humans don't have instincts. They avoid the hunters.

Because of their knowledge of vitality, most **Wo/man** are psychologically, physiologically and intuitively better inclined than most manly men and girly women for the job of keeping the culture on track to assure the survival of the species.

Male choice: confront the problem and kill off a bunch – brute force and ugliness.

Done and doing that and it's not acceptable nor is it effective.

Female choice: give birth to less children.

Doing that, quietly, efficiently and for the most part, painlessly.

Different message.

Both approaches are necessary and complimentary, but the **Wo/man'** method has a more lasting impact.

Why?

Because conceiving, carrying the fetus to term and finally birthing is an intensely personal experience that is only shared between the mother and the child and the lines of communication between them are established very early and they are intimate: i.e., subliminal.

When the links are established, nobody knows. I suspect that the timing varies from individual to individual.

In a perfect world the communication link would last throughout their entire lives, in reality it fades as the child grows and begins to reason.

I didn't say it was completely severed, I said it fades.

Big difference.

Simply put, **Wo/man** sense the vitality of human life more acutely than manly men and girly women and intuitively pass that information on to the next generation so they can adapt to new conditions and allow the species to survive while manly men try to force their will on the new conditions in the hope that their strength and intelligence will overcome the changing environment and allow the species to survive. Girly women make sure he dresses well.

In the long run the attempt at control generally fails.

Hence the more lasting impact.

OK, I've established that there is a danger (overpopulation) to the species (clan) that affects its ability to survive well, that **Wo/man** know of the danger more acutely than manly men and girly women and that **Wo/man** are taking actions (steps) to lessen the danger.

The steps that are being taken lessen the birth rate, which has the effect of allowing fewer of us surviving better with fewer resources.

What steps?

One is equality.

Actually equality is not a good descriptor because no two people are equal nor should they want to be. One can insist on equal protection under the law, and that's fine, but equality has such a…I don't know…Orwellian tinge to it.

Parity is a better word.

Social parity.

par·i·ty *n.* Equality, as in amount, status, or value.

See, much better. Status and value, that's what we're talking about.

This synthesis of achieving parity has not been completely achieved in the United States yet particularly from an economics point of view, but the problem is being worked.

This change in the accepted traditional customs and usages is progressing in some cultures more rapidly than others, but in those cultures where the new values have achieved a toe hold, the idea of parity of the genders is not only accepted, it has been ratified into law.

New rules are being developed.

The process of changing the thousands of years of tradition wherein the male is dominant and the female is submissive and of lesser value doesn't happen through legislation, although that's important, it happens at the mother's knee first. For several decades, mothers have been instructing their male and female children the rules of parity. How that is done varies from mother to mother and exactly what the rules are becoming is a little squishy, but it is being done and results are evident.

I don't think anyone can deny that the rules of engagement between the genders have changed. What was normal and accepted behavior for men is now viewed as boorish and often illegal. What was normal and accepted behavior for women is now viewed as frivolous and self-deprecating. The characteristics of sensitivity, compassion, respectfulness and active fathering are becoming valued behaviors in men while intelligence, strength, forthrightness and self-assuredness are becoming valued behaviors for women.

If you think that these changes are occurring because some legislator somewhere woke up one morning and decided that women have been getting the shaft and decided to rectify the situation, or that economics plays a major role, or that there is some magical vision, you are wrong.

The process of attaining parity, which is a huge cultural change, has taken centuries and is not yet totally complete. That process of change is almost totally controlled by **Wo/man**.

Whether we like it or not, the majority of children are raised by their own mothers. Stay-at-home dads, orphanages or other arrangements are a distinct minority. They all do a great job, but the majority determines the mores of our culture and the natal mothers raise the majority of children (adopted infants included).

Does this mean that mothers should stay at home to raise children?

Not at all.

Just the opposite, if the mother chooses.

The fact that a mother works and is a vital part of the community is a bit of cultural information that is transmitted to the child and teaches it parity.

The fact that dads assist or sometimes take the lead in this endeavor is also a bit of cultural information that is transmitted to the child and teaches it parity, but rarely does a child cry out for its dad when it falls and scratches a knee.

Does this mean that mothers who stay at home don't teach their children parity?

Not at all.

Just the opposite, if the mother chooses.

If the mother chooses!

Important stuff, choices.

As the mores change the mother can choose the *number* of children to birth.

Not the father, not the society, the mother.

Big difference.

How a mother makes that choice, nobody knows but women can only make that decision and make it stick if they have parity.

If a woman doesn't have veto power over the encroachment to her body then all bets are off and we are back to unrestricted population growth.

Not good.

Important stuff parity, because it assures that an individual has the right to choose and that right is not abrogated.

So how, exactly do mothers impart this parity information?

I'm not sure but I have an inkling.

All of us humans, men and women, operate within and react to our environment and each other in a very intuitive way. That is, we know things without actually thinking about them and we take action based on that "knowledge".

In the appearance arena, people, some better than others, have an intuitive knowledge gleaned at a very early age from parents, peers and role models of what "looking good" means and act on that knowledge to buy clothes, use makeup, diet, etc.

That is only part of the story.

When my wife bore our first child, she *intuitively* knew what to do. We read books and received advice, wanted and unwanted, but all that stuff only covers the approach, the details were hers and hers alone. She *knew* the details of acceptable behavior: when and how to comfort, when and how to ignore, when and how to correct, when and how to accept, etc. It was through those details that she passed on *her* culture and mores. Sure I had an input, but mine was intellectual while hers was subliminal. Also, her values were significantly different than her mother's.

Weird.

Not weird strange but weird awesome.

Mothers can sense the process of development in the child and through some wizardry, guide and instruct the child through the incredibly complex process of growing.

To me, one of the most fascinating aspect of the growing process is the learning of language, not just words and stringing the words together into sentences, but the connotation of the words and through those connotations the implantation into the child its view and understanding of its world.

Mothers teach the child the process of abstraction so that it can abstract and remove enough details to enable it to communicate. She teaches the child that an apple is round even though it isn't; that it is red even though it isn't and that there are many "rounds" and many "reds".

Sweetness is sometimes a problem.

What a wondrous and fascinating process it is for a child to evolve from an organism, which only responds to physical stimuli, to a sentient human as it starts to make sense of the grunts, wheezes, and clicks that we call speech. At first they perceive that the words are reality and act accordingly, but through their mother's guidance they come to understand that words *mean* all kinds of things.

"Hot, don't touch!"

Pretty simple statement, but to an infant, enormously complex.

Hot is not a thing but a state. Not all things have that state. Sometimes the same thing may not be hot.

Don't indicates some kind of action or inaction. What action?

Touch?

What the hell does that mean?

Tough stuff learning, and it boggles the mind that it happens at all.

You can read all the psycho and sociobable you want but each time a mother guides a reaching hand she is communicating something to the infant: yes, you can reach, no, you can't reach or it doesn't matter. That kind of instruction only comes from a mother and she does it thousands of times a day, mostly without thinking – intuition.

Through this guidance the mother teaches the infant parity and that it has options.

I might have implied that that there is some kind of mystical power in place that women are in tune with that whispers instructions on child rearing. I'm not going to discount that possibility and it would be fun to think so, but unfortunately more mundane forces are at work.

There is that little thing called logic and reason.

As the syntheses generated by the Woman, Movement began to take hold, **Wo/man** demanded and for the most part received legislative changes that began to level the playing field socially and in the work place. This leveling did not reduce male status, although a lot of men continue to whine that it has, it has had the effect of increasing woman's parity in the society.

As parity becomes more and more established, options that had never existed became available for women, options that have nothing whatever to do with family and children.

Mothers, by guiding the child, teach their children about those options

Don't ask me how.

I do know, however, that the techniques in terms of toy selection, play activities, reprimand methods, etc. are substantively different now than they were fifty years ago.

Maybe that's it.

I don't know.

The instructional process goes on for many years, but as the child grows and slowly expands its horizons the mother's influence wanes until the child becomes an adult and she has to let it go. Sure she continues to "parent" and worry and rejoice in the child, but her cultural transmittal job was really done in the first few years of infancy and would be forever be a part of who the child is.

Sometimes there are errors, but not very often.

Some children grow up to be jerks, or psychopaths or some other kind of malcontent but not very often.

Children are human and therefore not error free and thus some children misunderstand the mother's communications and grow up to be screwed-up adults.

Not the mother's fault.

You are jerk because you are flawed, possibly from birth, and your mother had nothing to do with it.

I have no idea why this is so and don't care, it just is.

If you think your flaw is significant, you can always visit your local shrink's couch.

Some, not many, mothers are jerks.

Tough break for the child.

Most, not all, children of jerks overcome.

I have no idea why this is so and don't care, it just is.

Some children don't have mothers or have mothers who have limited "mothering" ability and are only "cared for".

Some, not all but most, of these children grow up to be jerks.

Some children are subjected to war, genocide, famine and natural disasters more often than we would like.

How they will behave as adults, I don't know.

I suspect that most will be OK.

Obviously there are an infinite number of variables that affect the end result but mothers do their communicating thing in the first few years of infancy and after that it's pretty much a crapshoot.

Does education help this *initial* communication process?

Nope.

Actually it might be a hindrance because education may expose the mother to all the possibilities of error and get in the way of her intuition. No matter how educated you may be, every single new infant is, by definition, unique and does not fit the textbook models.

Information about food, hazardous chemicals, scheduling, abuse, etc. may be valuable, but the first time the child reaches, the books go out the window and intuition determines the mother's action.

That's why there is no such thing as a better mother; you are either a mother or just a breeder.

A breeder is a woman who is devoid of intuition. As a result, through action or inaction she places her child in harm's way. Basically, if you don't murder, abuse (physically and/or intellectually) or let someone else abuse the child, you're not a bad mother.

Physical abuse we understand pretty well but intellectual abuse is a little vague and the definition of what is and what is not intellectual abuse varies with time, place and community standards.

It's up to the mother and prevailing laws of the land.

Someone else may think you are doing a crappy job.

Too bad, they're wrong.

No matter how many times your mother or friends tell you are screwing up, they are wrong.

Is the child fed, clean and reasonably clothed; protected from rats, vermin or creepy crawly things; do you hug it, coo at it, snuggle with it, calm its fears and smile when it smiles; and lastly do you guide its reaching hands?

If the answer to all those questions is yes, then your intuition is working and you are a not a bad mother.

Period.

Don't have a $700 stroller?

Doesn't matter, the kid doesn't care.

Do you hug it and kiss away its tears?

It matters and the kid cares.

I know, I know, a bunch of people will say that there is more to mothering than the few things I mentioned and maybe there is but I think that the people that hold that view are just making the obvious more complicated than it needs to be.

An intuitive mother has discipline, some more than others, but a breeder has none. An intuitive mother knows that she is the absolute boss and determines the when, where and what. She also knows that a child is little more than a savage beast. It has no concept of cause and effect, no memory, no sense of time, minimal communication skills and virtually no empathy for anyone except for itself.

Not much to work with and the little beast is growing very rapidly.

Somehow she must teach it cause and effect, give it a memory, sense of time, the ability to communicate and impart into it the feeling of empathy toward others.

Only through discipline, hers and the child's, can those daunting tasks be accomplished.

Not reprimand discipline, but making order out of chaos discipline.

For instance, a child must be forced to sleep at regular intervals. A child who doesn't go to sleep at the same time every day is in a perpetual state of jet lag. There is a monumental amount of data being assimilated by the child and it must try to make sense of it all. A very difficult task and a child who is tired because of irregular sleep patterns will assimilate irregularly. That means that it will be confused and show its confusion through crankiness and hysteria.

In addition to the immense amount of data being assimilated, the child is undergoing physical changes. Its brain is ordering itself, new bone, muscle, nerves, ligaments, etc, are being formed at an astonishing rate. That's exhausting work and the little bugger needs regularity so all that growing can be done in an orderly fashion to maximize the child's potential.

Not to mention the fact that the mother needs a break now and then.

An intuitive mother says NO a LOT.

Does the child care?

Not really, because it knows that when things really get wacky mom will kiss the bubu to make it go away.

All mothers accomplish this task. Some have more peace in their homes than others; a few, very few, lose it and need some help and another few have children that remain, through no fault of her own, beasts forever.

In our modern society, mothers with their children are sometimes thrust into situations that are strange, bewildering, anxious and stressful.

The child howls.

People stare.

Is the child undisciplined?

Not necessarily.

Is the mother a poor mother?

Not necessarily.

She had no control of the when and where.

Sometimes situations just suck.

Period.

The fact is that the vast majority of children exhibit acceptable behavior, which proves that even though there are almost an infinite number of variations on disciplinary techniques, they all seem to work fairly well.

Even in the epitome of controlled chaos like Chucky Cheese or the local playground.

Back to education.

I find it difficult to believe that a highly educated and informed mother from Cleveland, for instance, is doing a better job of mothering than a mother from, I don't know, a farm outside of Nanking China. Their culture may be different but their child still reaches and the mother directs.

There is no evidence to support the presumption that the adult raised by that mother from Cleveland is somehow innately stronger, smarter, faster or in any way "better" than the adults raised by mothers from Nanking, Nairobi, Cairo or even some housing project in Atlanta.

The differences are only in the details.

If you don't agree with this, nock yourself out and go ahead and make life more complicated and read everything in those parenting magazines. They have a lot of good data that you can add to your intuitional repertoire,

Don't forget to buy stuff from the advertisements.

What I'm really sick of is the thousands of "experts" who are constantly telling moms what to do.

You go mom, and tell all these "experts", mostly men by the way, to blow it out their collective asses.

I'll stick with the fact that mothers have been doing this job for thousands, no millions of years, and not one single child has ever been born with an instruction manual yet mothers everywhere seem to be able to pull it off with an astoundingly high rate of success.

OK, **Wo/man** have a keener sense of survival than manly men and girly women. They sense that the survival of the species, or at least a lot of it, is in jeopardy and through their intuitive mothering skills are imparting to the next generation the necessary information for us to survive.

What information?

Don't have so many children, for one.

Sounds simple but there have been thousands of years of social pressure to do just the opposite and just saying no is not as simple as it seems.

To say no to social pressure and have the society listen requires that the person saying no have sufficient status in order to be heard.

Heard, understood and respected.

Therefore, one of the first steps to lowering the birth rate is for women to attain parity.

Without parity, the woman's voice is not heard, understood nor respected.

Lots of babies.

Catastrophe in the making.

With parity, women became able to educate the clan, tribe, society, nation and the species that women must perform all of the jobs required in order for the clan to survive well and that breeding and childrearing can no longer be THE job for women, but one of many.

Just like in Igor's time.

As the clan becomes educated to the reality that women are essential to the clan's ability to survive well and breeding and child rearing is no longer THE job for women, then having lots of babies minimizes the clan's options. Thus, many women are opting for fewer children and the clan, tribe, society, nation and the species will be able to survive better.

I don't know how an individual woman decides what the number of children she wants to birth but I suspect its part of that *feeling* thing I mentioned before. You know that fourth level of knowing - priorities.

We may think that parity between the genders is a new concept but it is, in fact, ancient and was/is essential to our survival.

Birth control pills were finally invented and contraception was/is pretty much OK, probably because it's a secret thing. A little pill in the morning and nobody knew. Of course the medical establishment, mostly men, made up all kinds of scare tactics about cancer and other horrible things, but that was/is mostly bullshit. The fact that using the pill regulated a woman's cycle, reduced cramping, cleared up skin blemishes and made a woman's life more manageable was of no interest. Now there are many devices and medicines that do the job that is best suited for each woman.

A significant number of the religious establishments also view contraception as a no-no, which is consistent with the idea that women are baby machines.

A lot of women's attitudes of the time were summarized by a lady friend of mine who was single (divorced) with three children: "If I have a choice between cancer and another child, I'll take cancer, thank you very much!"

Leading up to the time that the pill was invented, the total population was increasing at a very rapid rate. Medical science and sanitation was allowing people to live much longer than ever before. Longevity coupled with a fertility rate of about 3.6 caused the population to increase from about 2.5 billion in 1950 to 6.5 billion in just fifty years.

Thing were getting out of control and **Wo/man** worldwide sensed it.

They had to regain control of their wombs and slow down the birth rate. The only way to do this is to regain social parity.

Did any woman say this out loud?

Maybe not in so many words but they sure expressed it by action.

As economic and social parity began to be regained the next step to prevent catastrophe was to regain control of the womb – determine the number, if any, of children.

They had meetings.

"This is lion shit!" one of the ladies exclaimed.

I'm pretty sure that no one from NOW or Planned Parenthood said that, but you get the idea.

"Things are getting out of control and those stupid men have no idea what's happening."

That's probably a little closer.

"We must have equality before it's too late."

They said equality, but they really meant parity.

"Women and only women should decide on whether or not to give birth." They decided and chose contraception, vasectomies and tubal ligation as the most valuable tools in this effort.

Unfortunately the U.S. Supreme court did not agree and in 1936 classified any information about birth control as obscene. It wasn't until around 1965 that married couples could obtain contraceptives legally in all states.

Sounds quaint now, but then it was a big deal.

Unfortunately the U.S. Supreme Court still disagrees and has ruled that religious beliefs regarding female contraception trumps the law of the land thus sustaining the idea that a woman is merely a baby machine.

Occasionally, pregnancy occurs under circumstances that are not good.

Along comes Roe vs. Wade and everybody went nuts.

Like I said, contraception was mostly OK, but abortion?

Here's the problem that a lot of people, mostly manly men, can't seem to get their head around: social parity and control of the womb are digital issues. That is, you either have parity or you don't and a woman either has control of her womb or she doesn't.

You don't have social parity if there are exceptions; otherwise, by definition you don't have parity.

You don't have control of your womb if there are exceptions; otherwise, by definition, you don't have control.

Period.

Can an individual woman decide, for herself, that there are exceptions to parity or control?

Of course, that's her choice but she sacrifices parity.

Can someone else decide for her?

No!!!

Can she decide for someone else?

No!!!

As for manly men, it's none of our business.

First off, a manly man is not the child bearer, so he doesn't get a vote.

If, for some reason, he feels that he should have a vote on the issue of birth, his vote was to keep his pants zipped. Should some stupid jerk impregnate some young lady, the continuation of that pregnancy is her choice and her choice alone.

Manly men who argue to the contrary have no case, have no honor and let their King of Lust rule their reason.

Boo hoo!

Get over it and keep your pecker in its pants where it belongs.

You, mister manly man, are responsible for pregnancy.

Right now, in our culture, manly men get to skate because it seems that no matter what the circumstances; the female is somehow at fault.

Date rape?

Her fault.

Drunk?

Her fault.

Too much youthful passion?

Her fault.

The only possible exception to this social precept is if the female is a minor, and sometimes even that doesn't work.

All wrong!

Manly men can't have it both ways.

You can't pretend that you are the tough, macho guy, impregnate some lady and then get pissed because she decides to abort.

You can't pretend that you are the tough, macho guy, impregnate some lady and then get pissed because she decides not to abort and demands that you foot the bill.

You can't treat females like objects and then feign indignation when she doesn't demonstrate unbounded joy over the fact that you have just messed up her life and the life of a child yet to be born.

You can't pretend to be the leader, the boss and the not take the lead in protecting your lady from your little swimmers.

You can't whine about her responsibility for protection when you refuse protection for yourself.

You want to have sex?

Great. Then you, mister manly man, be absolutely certain that no pregnancy will result. Buy the pills yourself, if you have to, and wear a rubber.

No other alternatives are acceptable!

You can't have it both ways.

Besides, abortion is a last resort for a desperate situation. If men and women exercised some responsibility and used any one or several of the birth control methods available, then the entire issue of abortion becomes very close to being mute.

I also don't want to hear all this hocus-pocus about murder and all that tripe.

Murder is a legal term and as such it has conditionality. That is, there are degrees of murder and each degree has a certain penalty associated with it. Not all acts that result in a person's death are murder. Further, a death may occur and no one is held accountable. That is, the suspected perpetrator is found to be not guilty.

I didn't say innocent, I said not guilty. Just ask O.J. Simpson.

Prosecutors and law enforcers make mistakes all the time in both directions. Sometimes they bungle the case and the perpetrator goes without punishment and sometimes they arrest and convict the wrong person.

Complicated stuff murder.

Since murder is a legal term, the State (government) determines what is and what is not murder. That determination varies over time and place. Different nations have different rules at different times.

Many nations, dare I say most, have determined that the act of aborting is not murder in any circumstance. It may be illegal in some situations, but not murder. In fact, laws and customs restricting abortion are relatively new. Prior to the mid nineteenth century there were no laws on the subject.

Therefore, aborting is not murder from a secular point of view.

Besides, if abortion is murder in some degree, why isn't the shooter, the man, held accountable?

Now, from a religious point of view, things get a little murky.

For several thousand years, religions – pick one, I don't care – have codified rules designed to keep women subjugated for the express purpose of breeding more of the faithful or providing sacrifices to the gods.

Guess who runs the religions?

Manly men.

Big DUH there.

Religious faith can be a good thing. Religious faith is a powerful thing. Religious faith is consoling, uplifting, maybe even purifying and, for some, an excellent coping mechanism but on the subject of birth any relationship between an individual's faith and the rules established by organized religions is purely coincidental.

Your faith may tell you that children are a blessing and a gift from your God; the organized religion to which you belong doesn't give a damn.

It's a power thing.

When a man-priest stands up before his faithful and rants about the horrors of abortion he is talking to the women. Rarely does the man-priest stand up before the faithful and rant at the men in the congregation and demand that they use protection.

It's the woman who is about to murder the fetus.

The man...tish, tish, naughty boy.

When a man-priest stands up before his faithful and rants about the horrors of abortion he is expressing his fear. Not for the soul of the woman but the fear that he will lose control of his woman/women.

Pregnancy and birth have been the perfect states for him to exercise his dominance over women and the founders of all religions jumped on that state with both feet. Pregnancy creates a state of vulnerability, physically and mentally in a woman and birth, well, that's the big payoff. The woman must now care for the infant, thereby removing her from the field of competition and he can remain the boss.

Joan of Arc wasn't burned at the stake because she was some kind of witch, a heretic or some other weird descriptor; she was burned because she had become a political power and embodied the heresy that a woman could compete with men on an equal footing. To make sure that other women didn't take up the standard, kick ass and take names like she did, the myth that Joan was called upon by God was invented.

What a perfect ploy.

Lady, you want to compete with the boys?

God's got to tell you.

A bunch of women thereafter tried that but they were just burned before they got out of hand.

"Father Joseph, God spoke to me last night and said I should become an archer in the Kings army."

"Get thee to a nunnery!"

No wonder these man-priests, speaking for their organizations, are terrified. Birth is the last vestige of their power over women and in their terror they label abortion as a sin tantamount to murder.

What a crock!

It's a crock because all of the major religious organizations also give conditionality to murder.

Religions, like governments, also have definitions of murder. Most religious definitions are very similar to the secular definition and that stands to reason since some secular law evolved from religious law.

Some religions take a hard stand on the subject and refuse to participate in killing of any kind. Some Christians, Jehovah's Witnesses for example, refuse to participate in wars while some Hindus hold some animals sacred.

Most Christian religions don't take the "Thou shall not kill" commandment literally and condone killing under certain circumstances depending on time, place and affiliation.

Apparently there are conditions wherein killing someone is permissible.

Is there a list somewhere?

Naturally, if there is a list, then humans wrote it and it tends to vary with time and circumstance.

At some time it may have been permissible to kill heathens including women and children.

Ask the Native Americans or the Serbians or the French Huguenots.

Now? Not so much because the wrath of that terrible secular government will come down on your ass and lock you up.

In the future?

Who knows?

Society generally condemns the actions of zealots retrospectively, but at the time of the massacre, well, it seemed like a good idea.

Like I said, it gets a little murky and the rules governing what is and what is not murder are not written down and clearly defined by religions as they are in secular law.

Some interpretation is required.

Who does the interpreting?

It depends on the organization with which you are affiliated.

In most places, the choice of religious affiliation is more or less voluntary. That is, each person can chose the religion that most closely confirms their personal faith.

Whether faith comes before choice or choice brings on faith is immaterial. In any case the individual can choose.

"I used to be a Baptist but I converted to Islam."

Or whatever.

This movement of people from one religion to another is generally accepted and many religious organizations actively seek new recruits from other organizations and they have a sort of unwritten set of "rules" that governs the recruitment process.

For instance, it is generally considered to be in bad taste if some group kidnaps or blackmails people to sign up.

These "rules" exist to assure a more or less level playing field for all the competing factions as they struggle to gain recruits and prove that they are right and all others are wrong.

Another set of rules, based on the level playing field concept, is that one group can't impose its will on another group.

For instance, Methodists can't tell Catholics how and where to run their show and open criticism and ridicule is generally considered rude, crude and socially unacceptable.

That particular rule is backed up by a variety secular of laws.

Occasionally, some group or a coalition of groups gets a little confused and starts tinkering with the "rules" and try to impose their particular brand of correctness on everybody else.

That would be OK except that to do that they also have to tinker with the secular laws that prohibits one group from imposing its will on all other groups.

That's when the trouble starts.

In the United States, an amalgam of groups consisting primarily of conservative or rightwing Christians have formed a quasi-coalition calling themselves the Christian Coalition, the Moral Majority, the New Life Church and others. Whether or not the Christian Coalition or some other Evangelical Christian group is the leader of this loose arrangement or not, is immaterial. What is material is that their implied objective is to create, overturn or otherwise modify laws or Constitutional interpretations that they deem to be contrary to their views.

Some of the issues they focus on are prayer in school, teaching of evolution, display of religious icons in or on government facilities, etc.; others specifically target women like eliminating funding for Planned Parenthood and other clinics dealing in a woman's health, the teaching of sex education, dissemination of contraceptive information or devices, Roe vs. Wade, etc. The unspoken agenda for all of these attacks is to remove the concept of separation of church and state. Essentially rewrite the First Amendment to the Constitution thereby establishing a theocracy.

What the views of the majority of the populace are is not their concern.

"Not so!" They scream.

Of course it's so. What do you thing would be the effect if the majority of the members of Congress and the Supreme Court were Evangelical Christians?

Duh!

The sad thing is that the rank and file, who are emotionally attached to the "coalition", pay the bills and supply the votes, fail to see the danger and do not recognize the tactics of the leaders.

Tactics? What tactics?

I'm glad you asked.

Actually I'm not glad because discussing the tactics of mass movements would stray too far off of the subject, but if you want to find out how mass movements operate, Eric Hoffer's *The True Believer* is an excellent analysis of the subject.

Suffice it to say that the creating of an atmosphere of fear, suspicion and mistrust are some of the tactics.

You know, Christianity is under attack, our voice is not heard, the huge secular government is destroying our right to worship, judges are too "activist", etc., etc.

Sound familiar?

Very similar to the propaganda utilized by the Nazi's or the Communists in the last century.

Different target, same tactic.

Don't get your shorts in a bunch. I'm not implying that the Evangelical Christian movement is in any way similar to National Socialism; I'm just saying that the tactics are similar.

Still annoyed? Then you Mr. Evangelist – there are no Mrs. or Ms. of note – don't mess around in politics or you will suffer the indignity of being scrutinized like any other political movement.

As to Roe vs. Wade in particular, a variety of strategies are employed.

The first thing was to define a specific kind of murder; in this case that means abortion.

Apparently the new definition of a human is the instant some little sperm guy lodges himself in a female egg. Whether that takes place in a lab or by more conventional methods is immaterial. There is also a movement afoot called something like "personhood" that presumes that a human exists at the moment of conception or before and any interruption of that process is considered murder.

OK, now we have a fertilized egg and the new definition of this specific type of murder is anything that prevents that egg from potentially dividing and growing. That includes the "morning after pill" or any other tampering with the egg like stem cell research. I say potentially because there are bunches and bunches of the little buggers stashed in freezers all over the place that are never going to be used and are eventually discarded due to space limitations. Those guys fall under the same theoretical protection but it seems OK if they end up in a dumpster someplace rather than a lab for research.

Go figure.

There seems to be no conditionality to this position. That is, rape, incest, mental incapacity, drug abuse or any other condition where the woman was violated, abused or has a demonstrated incapacity to mother do not diminish the charge of murder.

She's pregnant; she must bear the child…after that …who knows?

Unfortunately, the evil secular State doesn't agree and apparently the majority of women don't either. The reason the State doesn't agree is that the set of cells that is dividing and multiplying inside the woman is just that, a bunch of cells. They cannot live without being where they are until they have matured to a certain point as specified by the law and science.

Got to ignore science and fix that.

Let's protest at clinics and embarrass, harass and otherwise make it difficult for women to get abortions.

Maybe kill a couple of doctors or revile them on the Internet.

Of course that's not murder, it's answering to a higher power.

Didn't work and got a lot of bad press.

Maybe we'll blow up or vandalize a couple of clinics.

Wrong again and more bad press.

Starting to look like kooks.

Besides the new definition of murder isn't selling.

What to do? What to do?

Aha! Let's get to the heart of the problem: got to overturn or modify Roe vs. Wade.

That's going to be tough and take a lot of time and cash.

Let's see…overturning or modifying Roe vs. Wade requires getting Supreme Court judges that we can influence. Getting a judge requires Congressional approval. Getting a judge appointed requires a President we can influence…and so forth.

First, invoke God by praying for the demise of a judge.

A pretty sure bet since they are all old.

Got to show everyone that you've got a direct line to the Boss.

Same logic that the old ladies used to calm the people when she knew that the storm was going to pass anyway.

At the same time, divert everybody's attention by creating a phony procedural issue in the Senate and sneak in a couple of judges.

Finally have a puppet President nominate an unqualified person, raise all kinds of smoke about it and then bring in a ringer.

A masterstroke. We'll see how it plays out.

See, in spite of all the rhetoric and posturing to the contrary, this movement, like all others, is really interested in power and uses the tools of dissention, diversion and subterfuge to achieve their goals. They wish to modify the current secular definition of murder to include a religious definition.

Once that is accomplished, they can then move on to all kinds of stuff.

Use your imagination – the sky is the limit.

Cromwell tried it in England (banning Christmas was one of his things) and several "modern" nations currently use religious law as the basis for their legal systems.

I know I've strayed from the main point, how restrictions on choice degrade a woman's parity, but I'm on a roll here, so bear with me.

If you think that the repeal or modification of Roe vs. Wade wouldn't be an intrusion into women's lives then you are living in Never Never Land.

The current interpretation basically says that the Government has no business interfering with a woman's choice to bring a fetus to term except for certain conditions.

What the Evangelical or fundamental Christians say is that the Government should insert itself into the process and make the decision for the woman.

If that's not intrusion, I don't know what is.

The most intrusive and dangerous concept being touted is the idea of Personhood. This idea states that as soon as an egg is fertilized that collection of cells is a person with the same rights and protection as any other citizen. That means that <u>any</u> interruption of the "growth" process of the fertilized egg can be considered murder.

So, we can have the condition that a woman miscarries at, let's say, twelve weeks, she can be charged with murder. She may not have known that she was pregnant but some cop decides that she engaged in "risky" behavior and she gets arrested and charged.

If you think that what I am saying is bullshit, look it up. There have been over 200 cases in the United States since the beginning of this century where exactly this has happened.

The thing that is really interesting about all of this is that women are the ones under attack.

What's up with that?

What about men?

Pregnant? Not your problem!

A woman gets impregnated and decides, for whatever reason, that she cannot bring the fetus to term so she aborts. Suddenly she's the pariah. Where is the man? Does he bear no responsibility?

Am I the only one that sees the ironic injustice to this?

As to the ladies who believe in the "right to life"…

That's your choice.

Of course if you really want to practice what you preach, line up at an abortion clinic and offer to adopt the child of every woman who enters.

Adoption too hard?

How about child support?

Still too hard?

Then I guess we'll let the woman abandon the baby and let it be raised by the state; unwanted, unloved and destined for a life of crime.

Guess what, dummy, you are still going to pay through your taxes.

At least you prevented a woman from murdering her child. The fact that the child will probably grow up and murder other people is not your concern.

Don't yell at me, check the probabilities.

Don't like that argument?

Too bad, because that IS the argument.

Crime has dropped in the United States by about 18% in the last decades while the age group that commits the most crimes, 16 to 30, has also dropped significantly.

Some of those children that weren't born were unwanted.

Is there a correlation?

Here's what I don't understand about the anti-choice folks.

If abortion is a no-no, then why not do everything in your power to prevent pregnancy in the first place?

Scream, cajole, preach to every man, woman and child that pregnancy can be prevented by the modern marvels of science.

Stand up in your pulpit and yell that if abortion is a sin, then not practicing contraception, of whatever kind, is a greater sin.

Obviously that's too hard.

It's too hard because abortion is not really the issue. The issue is the subjugation of women.

You see, as I have mentioned before, the only job that belongs exclusively to women is giving birth. You can't attack women because they might be a mechanic or a soldier, but you can attack them on the issue of pregnancy. If you can take away a woman's choice for abortion or contraception then you can force her into her most vulnerable state and you can be the master.

What is fascinating about this removing of choice thing is that many women are on that side.

Interesting, I wonder what that says about those women's psychological makeup? Do they like domination?

Hmmmm.

Oh well.

Giving birth is the easy part, rearing is the hard part. A human child is not a puppy. It is a complex organism that requires, in its early stages, undivided attention, guidance, counseling, affection, and care – constant care. Behavior must be taught, by example as well as by instruction. Safety, psychological as well as physical, is essential at all times…you've got the idea. You've read the books and watched the shows.

I have no idea, nor is it any of my business, what conditions exist in the mind of a woman who decides to abort, but one thing is obvious: she has decided that she is incapable of providing all of the energy required to supply the things I mentioned. She has decided, probably intuitively, that she is incapable of mothering or mothering more. This is a very important assessment because a child who is reared by a caretaker instead of a mother is rarely a complete human and in the final analysis an incomplete human will cause us all grief.

Are some women stupid and use abortion as a birth control technique? Yes.

Stupidity abounds everywhere and there's not much we can do about it except try and stop the man and woman from boinking without contraception.

Notice that I didn't say "incapable or unwilling" before. The reason should be obvious. There are a lot of women willing to breed who are incapable, which accounts for the army of caretakers who have to take children away from these "mothers" who neglect brutalize and often murder their children.

There seems to be some deeply ingrained almost mystical belief that if a woman is forced to give birth, she will somehow, magically perhaps, suddenly be imbued with the all the qualities of motherhood.

Unfortunately this is not the case.

Human women are not litter bitches. Instinct doesn't apply.

In the final analysis, ladies of the "right to life", if you believe that giving birth is an important definer of what a woman is, you are a champion of the concept that a woman is a life support system for a womb and a second class citizen.

You have chosen not to accept parity and control.

If you believe that, nock yourself out…

It's your choice.

If other women don't believe the same way, don't have them over for dinner.

It's your choice.

To prevent other women from aborting…

Not your choice.

To encourage, by action or inaction, the destruction of clinics and the assassination of doctors…

Obscene.

To pray for the death of a Supreme Court Justice so you can impose your will on others…

Disgustingly obscene.

Naturally, most people don't behave or feel that way anymore and I suspect that they never did. Most men and women have/had caring, respectful relationships with their spouses and children. Most men and women have/had established relationships wherein partnership and negotiation to achieve common goals are the hallmarks of the relationship.

Most men don't control their lady's womb and don't want to.

They may want a beer and a little nooky now and then, but control…I don't think so.

Rant time.

I'm going to rant a little bit and offer my personal opinion on some subjects that are more or less related to the general theme.

Artificial insemination.

Artificial insemination is a classic example of the baby machine mentality. Some people seem to be obsessed with the concept of perpetuating the "blood line" thing while ignoring the fact that we are all related.

Some women seem to think that being pregnant is the essence of motherhood.

Come on now, that's only nine months. Motherhood is for life. Pregnancy is only the incubation period. Besides, the initial stages may be exiting and awe-inspiring but soon thereafter there is nausea, back pain, bloated ankles, headaches, mood swings, etc. etc. not to mention the pain and discomfort of birthing.

All of that aside, since the goal is motherhood and you or your partner are having fertility problems, then adopt.

Think about it. You've got all that love, affection, compassion, tenderness and stuff welling up inside you, so share it with a child who is truly desperate for those attributes.

Adoption is the ultimate expression of your responsibility to the clan. You are demonstrating absolute control of your womb, mothering a child or children and not increasing the population.

You are saving the society from a neglected child who would otherwise grow up with a high probability of being dysfunctional.

You are a champion!

Further, let's say that you and your partner like large families. Then have two of your own and adopt three more.

A perfect solution.

Weddings.

There are three kinds of weddings: before a judge or Justice of the Peace, a quickie at someplace like Vegas or an elaborate affair. The last one makes me nuts.

An elaborate wedding with bridesmaids, groomsmen, ushers, etc. is a continuation of the Cinderella myth and degrading to the bride. It's degrading because "it's the Bride's day" as if she were to have no other day, which is exactly what used to happen in the "good old days". The groom has no real function on this particular occasion and he dare not express an opinion on anything or suffer the wrath of the bride and her mother – assuming they haven't bitched each other to death yet. The bride's father is supposed to pay for the whole shindig, which is an extension of the dowry thing presuming that the groom has to be paid to take the girl in the first place.

It's disgusting, expensive, stressful and meaningless.

The party afterwards, however, is cool and a proper celebration of the start of a very proper relationship. The honeymoon is also cool.

Bachelor parties also suck!

Enough said on that, now on to marriage.

For a man to choose to father a child without that little civil nicety called a marriage license is more than just rude and insensitive; it's cowardly and dishonorable.

There is absolutely no acceptable argument to the contrary.

For a woman to allow herself to be impregnated without that little civil nicety called a marriage license is more than just rude and insensitive; it's cowardly, dishonorable and stupid.

We are talking about life and death decisions here and...

There is absolutely no acceptable argument to the contrary.

"But..."

But nothing!

Screw around all you want to, but do not allow pregnancy to occur. This is the twenty first century, you idiot, and pregnancy does not necessarily have to follow screwing.

Except for financial issues, the marriage license is not important to the adults. The child is who is important. You know, little stuff like legitimacy, continuity and the necessary paperwork to establish one's identity.

Not important? Not your call, it is the child's call.

Getting married and then deciding to have a child indicates some degree of planning and marshaling of resources. Getting pregnant without marriage indicates accidental behavior and lack of planning. Some would call that sort of thing immature, I call it stupid and that's just the beginning because the support resources will have to come from someone else – a continuation of stupidity.

Further it is degrading to the woman because she is always the "girlfriend" which has, at best, the connotation of childlike or at worst a mistress or kept woman even if she is paying the bills.

Incidentally, you might want to look up the IRS rules about illegitimate children and who gets to deduct what.

The death penalty.

It's a pain in the ass.

It's a pain because the system that gets someone on death row is not error free.

It's a pain because the process is expensive.

It's a pain because a whole lot of people spend a lot of time and energy debating, ranting and raving and in general being obnoxious.

It's a pain because the issue allows some political Mogul the opportunity to pretend that he/she is tough on crime while she/he fleeces the taxpayer in countless ways.

It's a pain because there doesn't seem to be an upside to the whole thing.

Just do away with it and save those of us that don't care one way or the other a lot of grief.

Related to the death penalty is the concept of closure.

Closure, as the term it is currently used, smells a lot like revenge.

Revenge is also a pain in the ass.

It's a pain because the initial damage is not repaired.

It's a pain because it is self-perpetuating and consuming.

It's a pain because whatever satisfaction is derived is temporary at best.

It's a pain because we confuse revenge with justice.

It's a pain because it does not allow the injured party to forgive which is one of those processes that Homo sapiens developed to assure our survival.

Sex.

Sex annoys me. Not the act, that's a lot of fun, but the emphasis our society, primarily the Moguls, place on it. Sex, sexuality, sexiness permeates almost every facet of our current culture, from washing machines to dildos. Sex, or the image of sexiness is a huge marketing tool for almost every product we can think of and its use seems to work. We spend upwards of five billion dollars a year on a variety of tools designed to enhance the act.

It's annoying.

Men are caricatured as ogling, raging Tasmanian Devils spreading their seed willy-nilly and women are either victims, enticers or willing accomplices.

Just ask *Cosmopolitan*.

Have we lost our collective minds?

Have we completely forgotten that intimacy is the goal?

Intimacy means personal connectivity, compassion, understanding, empathy and hundreds of other feelings that one human has for another regardless of gender. Intimacy is established over time and may or may not lead to sex. Sex without intimacy is sweaty, short, shallow and usually not satisfying. Sex resulting from intimacy is usually good and often spectacular.

Almost all species have sex. Humans are the only species that intellectualizes about it. We have all kinds of fantasies and forget that the body organs can't keep up with the mind.

We treat sex as if it were some kind of drug. The first few times you get a great high and then it wears off and you spend a great deal of time, effort and money to try to recreate the sensation, but inevitably fail. With chemical drugs you eventually die, with non-intimate sex you destroy relationships.

The other part of sex that's annoying is that we are led to believe that the continuous quest to boink is "natural". Apparently, we have no intellect and are prisoners of our genetic makeup. Thus, men are destined to forever be Tasmanian Devils and women victims or seductresses.

What a crock!

The "natural" thing implies instinct. We don't have any. We make up for our lack of instinct through intimacy. The compassion and empathy humans have for one another is the key element of our survival. Thus, horniness can be controlled. Not so much when we are young, but as we age and gain experience we can learn to control every aspect of our behavior. Shrinks have all kinds of fancy words for those who are incapable or unwilling to control their behavior.

So let's de-emphasize the act of sex or the state of sexiness and emphasize intimacy.

It'll be tough for the Moguls since they are interested in a quick buck and don't care who gets trampled.

Rant over.

Now on to parenting.

Not a real job, you say.

Wake up and smell the coffee, I say.

First off, parenting is the single most important job in the world, quite possibly the most difficult and certainly has the potential to be the most rewarding.

Question: If the future of the species and quite possibly the planet rests on the shoulders of the next generation, then why does society consider child rearing less than important?

"Child rearing is important."

Horse pucky. Tell that to the boss when a deadline has to be met, a war to be fought, a crime to be solved or a fire to be put out. In our society, business or political pressures always take precedent. As a result, the general populace has difficulty prioritizing family over business and it is often made clear that if one should prioritize family they will be less "successful". Then, it is assumed, that if you are less "successful" income will be lower and they will have limited access to the educational and social amenities to allow their children to attain their full potential.

Is that last socio-babble sentence true?

Nope.

Why?

The opposite is true because parents who prioritize family over business assure that their children will have access to the most valuable educational and social amenity available – care, love and attention.

Is financial and business success a hindrance to effective child rearing? Nope.

Lack of attention, particularly in the preteen years, is. If the parents provide attention and guidance during the preteen years, there is a higher probability that the child will survive as a teenager and become a contributing adult.

So there you have it. A social dichotomy.

Everybody knows that the teenager of today will be the adult of tomorrow and wants those budding adults to "carry the torch" of civilization. Some don't want to admit it and cringe at the prospect, but know it nevertheless. On the other hand, the society refuses to allocate the necessary resources (money, time, support) to try to increase the probability of success.

The "solution" to this dichotomy has been to relegate the job, almost exclusively, to women.

Notice that I used the word "relegate" as opposed to assign or delegate. The latter two words connote thinking as in having a list of tasks and doling them out to appropriate personnel. Relegate implies an inferior task. Something meted out with the wave of the hand as if its performance were somehow demeaning or inferior.

Subtle difference perhaps, but critical and interesting.

For as long as we can remember women have been second-class citizens, deemed to be incapable of the simplest managerial task, yet we have consistently entrusted the future of the species to this supposedly "inferior" being.

Am I the only one that sees the irony in this?

Seriously weird.

Even the feminist sisters put down the task: "Men are pigs. They leave us with the dirty diapers, laundry or whatever. We're not going to take it anymore. We're going to subcontract the task. Nobody will call me a stay-at-home mom!"

It's very hard to get your head around this bit of weirdness.

You might say: "OK, I'll concede that parenting is an important job but it's not an IMPORTANT job like that of a lawyer a fireman or an executive."

Oh really?

First off, you can't compare the jobs of lawyer, fireman, butcher, baker and candlestick maker to a mom's job (gender is immaterial, fathers are just male moms) because they are all employees and must do their master's bidding; a mom has to run the show. Even if you are self-employed, the comparison doesn't fit because you have to be responsive to your customers. A mom has no customers in the traditional sense.

"What do you mean, 'in the traditional sense'?"

People who are employed produce products. A lawyer's product is a successful litigation or contract or merger or some such "thing" that is measurable and for which the lawyer receives compensation. His/her clients are her/his customers and they thrive or fail depending on how well the lawyer performs his/her job. The people who manufacture things have customers who purchase the thing and, hopefully, they will be satisfied and purchase more things.

A mom's product is a "well adjusted", productive adult member of society and in that sense his/her customer is the society.

An executive's customers are the stockholders, the employees, the product's consumers, in short, the society.

Same as mom's.

Not only are the customers of the executive and mom similar, the functions are similar.

Let's do a comparative analysis.

Management consists of planning, organizing, directing and controlling. There are a whole lot of sub divisions to these basic tasks but most of them are buzz words designed to make management consultants sound like they know something.

1. Planning
   - Executive

     She/he plans budget allocations based on limited (as opposed to infinite) resources to produce the product and maximize the profitability of the firm. To accomplish this task, he/she has experts with extensive training to provide guidance and options.

- Mom

  She/he plans budget allocations based on limited (as opposed to infinite) resources to produce the product and maximize the profitability (savings) of the firm (family). To accomplish this task he/she has <u>no experts</u> to provide guidance and options and little or no training of her/his own.

2. Organizing
   - Executive

     Marshals all the requisite resources such as people, facilities and machinery to accomplish the plan.

   - Mom

     Marshals all the requisite resources such as people (husband, wife, grandmother, baby sitter, teachers, doctors, etc.), facilities (home) and machinery (washer, dryer, other appliances, car, etc.) to accomplish the plan.

3. Directing
   - Executive

     Directs the allocation of resources to execute the plan.

   - Mom

     Directs the allocation of resources to execute the plan.

4. Controlling
   - Executive

     Monitors the progress of the plan and, with the assistance of experts, makes the necessary adjustments to the execution of the plan to "stay the course".

   - Mom

     Monitors the progress of the plan and, with the assistance of experts (husband, wife, grandmother, teachers, doctors, literature, etc.), makes the necessary adjustments to the execution of the plan to "stay the course".

Same job, just matters of degree, but moms get no vacations, time off or pay. I contend that the job is more difficult, but the society obviously disagrees.

Society obviously disagrees with the childcare thing as well.

If we can all agree that the child of today will be the adult of tomorrow (say in twenty years) and that adult will work, lead, follow or otherwise run the society and make whatever systems are in place work including taking care of those pesky old folks, then it follows that for the benefit of the perpetuation of society or even the species, that child should be given the maximum opportunity to succeed i.e.: be a contributing non-criminal or not display some other social pathology.

Obviously we don't take that position.

Instead we take the position that childcare assistance for a working mom (again, gender is immaterial) is some kind of a perk.

"If she wants to have children, she should stay home where she belongs!"

Splendid.

Let's have every woman of childbearing age who might or already has children not work.

The economic ramifications of that approach would be devastating.

I'm not only talking about "career" women with tons of education, but also about the millions of women from police officers to restaurant servers; from clinicians to housekeeping staff; from retail clerks to security guards; etc. The millions of women who make our economy what it is. I am also talking about single dads or husbands who are not the primary breadwinners, the millions of dads who are invisible and get no credit for their contribution to the rearing of the next inheritors of the earth.

Childcare and the related support systems for working and non-working moms is not a perk for her or him – it is a necessity. Not only for the moms and the economy but also for the children.

Most of us live surrounded by thousands or perhaps millions of people. We have just begun to realize that the world, the society and the geology, is an enormously complicated and often dangerous place. Unknown opportunities and hazards lurk at every crossroads yet we ignore that the future of society thrives or fails depending on how the moms collectively do their job and we refuse to divert sufficient resources to provide even the most meager assistance to assure their success.

We just don't give a shit.

"That's a bit of a stretch."

Oh really?

Let's assume that all the moms taught their children that the color of a person's skin determines that person's value…oops, done that already.

Let's assume that all the moms taught their children that a woman's place is in the home and snagging a good provider is all she should aspire to…oops again.

Let's assume that all the moms taught their boy children that ambition, athleticism, leadership, competitive, etc. are the necessary requirements for people with penises and affection, cheerfulness, quiet, gentleness, etc. are necessary requirements for people without penises…oops done that and doing it now.

Not to mention sexy and attractive or manly and strong.

"Big boys don't cry."

"What a pretty little girl."

Moms are the purveyors of the society's values. From birth they teach their children "correct" and "incorrect" behavior, language and attitudes and, just like women with their clothing choices that can cause financial catastrophe, if moms decide that a certain behavior or value is "incorrect" or just passé, that value is implanted in the next generation. It may take several generations to take effect, but take it will and society evolves.

Support systems like childcare only increase the possibility of success.

"But children, especially teenagers, rebel and make up their own values."

True, but not universally and more often than not you'll hear: "Jeez, I sound just like my mother!"

There may be a presumption that I am talking about education. There is Education and there is education.

Education (upper case) is performed by a variety of public, private and home schooling school systems. The purpose of these systems is to organize and impart information to the student using a variety of techniques in the hope that the student will assimilate the data, make sense of it and eventually utilize it as required. An acceptable standard is a passing grade, which means that the student *seems* to have assimilated 70% of the data.

All of these systems do an amazingly good job. Some better than others, but that is pretty much a judgment call.

The reason that I say that they do a good job is because if the assumption that the IQ score is a measurement of an individual's intelligence and the distribution of intelligence follows a Gaussian distribution is correct, then half of the population has an IQ score of less than 100, the standard.

If this is true, then the fact that over 80% of the population has completed the curriculum for high school is an amazing achievement since the number should be around 50%.

You can argue among yourselves.

Education (lower case), the implantation of values, priorities, affection, respect and the thousands of other things that make up a person is performed by the parent(s) prior to formal education and continually reinforced as the child grows.

Important stuff, education (lower case) and is the key to how the society behaves.

Also there seems to be no agreement whatsoever on the details of how or what education to provide but, if you look at the results over the centuries, they have been astoundingly successful. There are over seven billion of us, all unique, and yet we survive, laugh, play, love, hate, cry, dream, etc. with amazing similarity and in reasonable harmony.

Only **Wo/man** that are connected could provide this degree of homogeneity across thousands of miles, a myriad of different cultures, competing religious system and governments which do better at oppression than nurture.

So Mr. or Ms. Mogul, when you get old and don't want to be set out on a flat rock and eaten by wolves when the next generations take over, I suggest you pay attention and start providing assistance to moms and dads because **Wo/man** everywhere are attacking, discarding or generally ignoring the rule.

Eight

The Youth Revolution

Time marched on and women were pretty much screwed but as the Late Middle Ages started (around the year 1300 more or less) something strange started to happen. Art and literature started to come on the scene. Books were being written that had nothing to do with religion. Books in prose and verse about knights in shining armor, chivalry and some semi-porno stuff. The most famous was Chaucer's Canterbury Tales.

His stories glorified knighthood and told of fair damsels, true love and the purity of womanhood. People who could read lapped it up and those who couldn't read heard the stories from minstrels at fairs or inns or other social gatherings. The fact that most of this stuff was bullshit was totally beside the point; it was entertaining.

A new view of women was emerging. Chivalry was invented and women were put on a pedestal, more or less, and as Erica Jong put it:

Women are the only exploited group in history that has been idealized into powerlessness.

Things stayed that way for a long time but because of the idealization, the oppression of women began to slacken and many women began to emerge as serious contributors to science, art, literature and politics.

Eventually there was a revolution in the 1960s.

Here's what happened.

Back in the day, three hundred or so years ago, there wasn't a lot of money to go around. Aside from a lot of crappy rules imposed by England, money was one of the prime motivators for the U.S. to become a nation. Soon the new nation was expanding and building. Manufacturing was the thing, along with transportation, mining, textiles, construction and other "heavy" industries. Farming was also a big thing, employing about 30% of the population. Most of the dough was in the hands of the "leaders" of industry or Robber Barons as they were sometimes called. In 1905 there were about 83 million people in the U.S. and the Moguls knew that the population was increasing and they wanted to get as much money from the folks as they could. Most of the big guys, steel, railroads and the government, didn't think much about the folks, soon to be known as consumers (a term first used by Adam Smith in 1784), but a bunch of guys did.

The clothing guys, the medicine guys, the beverage guys, the household appliance guys, etc. – the retail people; those guys thought about the folks a lot and were constantly coming up with new stuff to sell but they were pretty much small potatoes until near the end of the nineteenth century.

Along come Edison and Tesla. Both of these guys wanted to provide electricity to the masses. Each one had a different technique and a battle ensued between alternating current and direct current or AC and DC (not the band). AC (Tesla – actually Westinghouse used Tesla's idea) won but Edison got the credit. In any case, electricity became available to everybody and as more households were hooked up, it became cheaper. By the 1940s a house without electricity was a rarity.

Because of electricity, new kinds of businesses sprung up all over the place. Washing machines, irons, sewing machines, toasters and electric shavers were being hawked and the consumers were buying. Neat inventions came along like Teflon, nylon, the ballpoint pen and the automatic bread-slicer (1928).

"Automatic bread-slicer? How is that an important invention?"

Everybody knows you can't make a peanut butter and jelly sandwich without sliced bread.

Where do you think the expression, "That's the greatest thing since sliced bread", came from?

Very important invention!

Anyhow, stuff was being developed, manufactured and sold to make the lives of the consumers easier. Easier lives meant some free time and free time meant time to think and thinking produced more inventions.

Some of the stuff being invented had a dual purpose; it could be used for recreation and to conduct business. Transportation and communication became big business. First came railroads, then airplanes then airmail; telegraph then telephones, cars then roads, then highways, motels, Howard Johnson's and …you've got the idea.

The whole idea of recreation being an industry was evolving. Up until the twentieth century, recreation and fun was pretty much a rich thing. Workers didn't have much time or money to indulge in anything but work except for Sundays or holydays. The occasional picnic or harvest festival for the rural folks or bars and saloons for the city folks was pretty much it.

Suddenly people had more dough and time. In addition to gadgetry to make everyone's life easier, things were being invented to make a buck off of the free time. Things like movies, talking movies, movies in color, comic books, comic strips, radio, amusement parks, hot dogs, hamburgers and eventually television.

A lot of stuff happening in a very short time.

The nation had pretty well divided itself into two camps: managers and workers. Managers are people who run things, govern and invest money to make money, hopefully a pile of it. Workers are pretty much wage earners, farmers and Mom and Pop businesses. Workers invest money too, but they do it for nest-egg purposes, not as a primary source of income.

Both camps wanted the same thing but didn't know it. The managers wanted the people to buy their stuff and the workers wanted to earn enough money so they could afford to buy the stuff.

Everybody wanted the same thing.

Could they reach an agreement?

No.

Still can't.

Then, as now, management has no historical knowledge. They are so focused on their short term Return on Investment (ROI) that they have forgotten that workers don't save; they spend. If wages don't increase but costs go up; consumers stop spending. When consumers stop spending everybody goes nuts and blame the recession, depression or whatever on something else; it's the Democrats; it's the Republicans; it's illegal immigrants; it's out-sourcing. But secretly we know it's the Chinese or the Japanese or maybe it's those guys from India, we've always known that they were sneaky little devils – you know, brown skin and all.

Horse pucky!

Management is ALWAYS responsible for the economic condition.

Marx knew this and he and Engels invented Communism but they ignored or misunderstood a couple of things. The first thing they ignored was that workers are all wanwbe managers. Everybody wants to own things and become rich. Another thing was that they, and all who believed in their brand of manure, misunderstood the essence of revolution. They said it right: thesis, antithesis and synthesis, but they thought that through economics or economic structure the synthesis would be a better life for everyone[1].

ARRRP!

WRONG

"Workers of the world. Unite!"

Unite to do what?

More work?

Fortunately they were so wrong that the whole system collapsed.

Back in the USA management wouldn't give the workers a break, so the workers formed unions.

A lot of bloodshed.

As an example, Henry Ford, that icon of American Industry, recognized that if he didn't pay his workers, they couldn't afford to buy his cars but he was so rabidly anti-union that he posted machine gunners at his factories to keep union organizers out.

He was one of the good guys, even though several people were gunned down by his "troops".

Finally, unions got their way, laws were passed and the dough started to get spread around.

In spite of all the dire predictions, management started raking in money by the ton (I told you these guys aren't too bright).

---

[1] There's a lot of argument as to whether Marx first used the terms, but it doesn't matter because in the general mind he's blamed for it.

1914 -- World War I.

How 'Ya gonna keep 'Em down on the farm? (After they've seen Paree?)

Cute song written in 1918 that embodied the fact that "tha times they are a changin'".

1929 – The stock market crashed The Great Depression came and nobody had any dough. World War II came and money was being redistributed rapidly and people wanted to buy stuff. Retail and Service started to become major industries.

1945 – World War II ended and the United States was the Victor with a capital V.

No longer did the sons have to work the fields of the family farm to help support the family. Sons of fathers who were miners or steel workers came back from the war and decided that they wanted to do something else, like get an education.

The GI bill.

Women who had worked in the factories during the war had discovered that they could wield a welding machine with the best of them.

Change was in the wind.

Actually, by the 1950s, tremendous changes had taken place in the previous fifty years, but the impact of those changes had not become an integral part of the American psyche. That means that most of the people had not begun to behave differently. Most people still cherished the values of their parents. Sure there were a lot of gadgets, people generally had more disposable income (economist-speak for money you spend instead of saving) and the quality of life for most Americans after the war was better than anyone could have imagined twenty years ago.

The Protestant Ethic was in full force. God rewards those who work hard and a live "pure" life was the underlying theme that governed most people's lives. I put "pure" in quotes because the idea of purity had limited scope and was defined by a select group who happened to be in the majority, primarily White Anglo-Saxon Protestants, WASPs.

Why wouldn't they believe? They had tangible evidence that God was smiling on them: cars, houses, good jobs and Eisenhower was President.

Sounds fair to me.

Of course everyone who wasn't a WASP, including women, was left out of the whole thing.

Change was in the wind and no one could see the storm coming.

Social change doesn't happen instantly; it kind of creeps along until one day you wake up and discover that your world has changed. That's exactly what started to happen in the fifties.

People were waking up and saying: "Whuaaa?"

I'm not going to launch into a big dissertation on all the stuff that happened in the fifties, sixties and seventies; you can do that on your own, but attitudes about children were changing and those attitudinal changes were the root causes for all the stuff that followed.

One perception that was changing was that education rather than household chores should be the primary occupation for children. Parents and the law were insisting that children go to school. In the 1930s and 1940s many young boys and girls were the first members of their families to be graduated from high school and it was a big deal. Such a big deal in fact that parents were adjusting their life to assure that the graduation would take place and the "teenager" was invented (a term first written in a Canadian publication in 1921).

Another attitude change was that children were no longer viewed as possessions.

Both of these ideas had been brewing for a long time, but in the forties and fifties we woke up and found out that it was so.

To give you an example, my grandfather never forgave my father for leaving the farm to get an education in the 1920's while my father would have never forgiven me if I hadn't obtained an education. For girls in my family it was a little slower. My aunt never was allowed to leave the farm to complete high school, household chores being the only suitable endeavors for girls, but escaped by eloping in the 1930s and later made a pile of money hauling trash.

So there you have it. My father was considered a possession by his father but I was not my father's possession, and likewise my aunt does not own her daughters even though she was owned by her father. Of course her liberation was ten years later.

By the fifties, thousands of years of tradition regarding a child's status in life was not only passé, it was frowned upon. The "ordinary" people now viewed their children as "members of the family". Before the twentieth century, unwanted children (read: noncontributing or excess) of ordinary people were sold, given away or otherwise disposed of. As the eighteenth and nineteenth centuries ticked along and the twentieth century dawned, the concept that children were commodities slowly evaporated. Child labor laws were passed (1938) and the concept of "what's best for the child" began to take precedence over the parental interest and rights. Families that got rid of or "aborted" their children became pariahs.

The society was creating a monster, not a Monster, but a monster just the same and teenager was its name.

Films, comic strips and literature depicting the antics of children became popular. Children became lovable to everyone with the possible exception of W.C. Fields, the comic movie actor, who declared: "Never work with children or animals".

Storytellers like Charles Dickens and Mark Twain were writing books about children and the public was identifying with the plight of the characters.

The reason this all happened was the redistribution of wealth. As money became spread around, people began to realize that the way things were did not necessarily mean that they had to stay that way. The possibility of a better life in the future started to become something people could envision.

A little money in your pocket and you could start to hope. Maybe not for yourself so much, but for the extension of yourself: your children.

Hope springs eternal…

Ordinary women started to PREPARE and workers said: "This is a load of crap" and formed unions whose whole impetus was a better future. The early organizers and rank and file took enormous risks so that those that followed could work and live better.

Politicians, wanting to get elected, got with the program and passed laws with the future in mind. Social Security, the GI Bill and many of the New Deal programs were not laws designed to fix the now, rather to make the future better.

Laws were passed requiring that all children, regardless of gender, attend school. Farm work and household chores became secondary or even tertiary in the hierarchy of important duties for children.

Millions of immigrants came and are still coming, hopefully to make their life better but definitely to make their children's life better.

So, in a sense, our hopes for a better life were invested in our children.

Children were/are endowed with a sanctity unparalleled in the history of western civilization.

Suddenly children became the focus of the family unit. Providing the best possible atmosphere for children became paramount.

Doctor Spock preached his child rearing techniques to millions of families and his emphasis was not on discipline, but on nurturing.

Along with the concept of nurturing came the idea that children should be paid for performing the few trivial household chores assigned to them and the idea of an allowance was born. By 1963, 50% of the professional households had some form of allowance for their children.

Notice that mothers weren't paid, only the children. It would take fifty years and a couple of clever divorce lawyers to rectify that discrepancy.

The Moguls had children who had allowances and knew that their children wanted to spend that money. A plan was set in motion to get that money. The Moguls also knew, from the experiences with their own children, that the children's lust for more of an allowance was insatiable. Their children would whine, beg, cajole or whatever to get a toy just like Johnny's down the street, and the Moguls would acquiesce.

In the "good old days" the parent would have just whacked the kid and told him to shut-up. Now the parent was suddenly negotiating and nurturing.

Television

Aha: a tool by which more products can be advertised and sold. Radio and comics had started the ball rolling, but television with PICTURES?

Holy Allowance, Batman! Let's make shows geared to the family and to children and pimp our products.

Howdy Doody, Mr. Rodgers, Captain Kangaroo, Cecil the Serpent and cartoons, plenty of cartoons.

"Hey kids! What time is it?

"It's Howdy Doody time and don't forget to get your box of XYZ cereal with the secret decoder ring."

"Mommy, Mommy can we get a box of XYZ cereal? Pleeeese?

"No Billy, we eat oatmeal for breakfast."

"Ptooey! Oatmeal tastes like mush. I want XYZ cereal! I'll eat it all! Pleeese! Pleeeese?

"Oh alright, but you have to eat it all. Remember breakfast is the most important meal of the day."

Little decoder ring in hand, Billy was happy, peace reigned in the household and brand name identification was in place. Little Billy would grow up and eat the same crap for breakfast and have bypass surgery at fifty-five.

By the fifties, behavior in children that would not have been tolerated a short thirty years ago was now normal and the Moguls knew it and got rich.

For the first time ever, we started labeling a whole generation of children: Post-war Babies, The Me Generation, Baby Boomers, Generation X, etc.

The idolization of children was in full swing!

Parents, of course, were spending their money on other things like, mortgages, appliances and stuff like that.

Boring!

Parents of the children in the 1950s were born either just before or during the Great Depression. They had fought and suffered through the Great War. They had suddenly acquired a fair amount of wealth. New lifestyles (suburbia) were emerging, new products, new mobility, new jobs, new everything: Communism, The Bomb, air travel, cars for everyone, TV, air conditioning, Technicolor, instant news, etc., etc.

A lot to cope with and no road map.

The only thing they knew for sure is that they didn't want to treat their children as their parents had treated them, but they didn't really know how to pull it off.

Trial and error was/is the norm.

The parents had unleashed a monster and how we navigate in the world will never be the same. The babies of the 1950s grew to adulthood better educated, more pampered and with more money than any other generation in history. Along with the pampering, money and education came more free time.

What happens when you have more free time?

You think.

And think they did.

Young people throughout the world thought about all kinds of things that did not occur to their parents and they asked why? They questioned the why of almost everything: bigotry, the validity of war, dress codes, health, marriage, sex, drugs, love, relationships, religion, wealth and just about everything else that anyone could think of.

Leaders emerged and voiced the attitude:

Bobby Kennedy said:

"Some people see things as they are and they say why. I dream of things that never were and ask why not?"

There were no answers, no one to ask, and no one to trust.

They made up answers as they went along.

Was this generation homogeneous? Did they all think, act or perceive the same way? Of course not, but these young people, and there were a bunch of them (70 million or nearly half of the population), had one unifying ethos: music.

Elvis, The Beatles, The Who, The Rolling Stones, Joan Baez, Dillon, Joplin and Hendrix to name a few, provided the music and lyrics that struck a chord in the hearts and minds of millions. They sang about bigotry, the validity of war, dress codes, health, marriage, sex, drugs, love, relationships, religion, wealth and everything else that was on the mind of those same millions.

A song by Helen Reddy kind of says it:

> I am woman, hear me roar
> In numbers too big to ignore
> And I know too much to go back an' pretend
> 'cause I've heard it all before
> And I've been down there on the floor
> No one's ever gonna keep me down again.
> Oh yes, I am wise…
> I am strong…
> I am invincible…
> I am woman.

The Moguls went nuts. Television exploded. Advertising exploded. Money poured in by the truckloads. The parents sacrificed and scrimped to pay for their children's whims.

The over 40 crowd became a specialized marginal market (big ticket items like houses, appliances and upscale cars). All the rest of the dough went to the kids. The 18 to 30 crowd was the one to cater to. Besides, the stuff the young wanted to buy had/has a significantly higher profit ratio (margin) and was/is almost instantly obsolete.

Let's recap. A significant percentage of the world population was between 16 and 30 years old. They had money and time to think. Because of the thinking, they were questioning their parent's values (mores) and the mores of society at large.

I used the word mores, not morals. There is a significant difference.

mo·res *pl., n.* The accepted traditional customs and usages of a particular social group that come to be regarded as essential to its survival and welfare, thence often becoming, through general observance, part of a formalized legal code.

mor·al *adj.* Of or concerned with the judgment of the goodness or badness of the human action and character; pertaining to the discernment of good and evil.

Mores is a noun and moral is an adjective thus we can say that some mores are moral and others are immoral based on ones perception of good or evil.

Mores are accepted customs and usages *essential to its (social group) survival and welfare.* Very little to do with good and evil.

"Spare the rod and spoil the child" was an accepted custom and usage and thought to be good; now…not so much (welfare).

"A woman's place is in the home" was an accepted custom and usage and thought to be good; now…not so much (economic and psychological survival).

A lot of mores that have nothing to do with good and evil; for instance: saying please and thank you (welfare), breast feeding (welfare), driving on one side of the road (survival) or washing ones hands (welfare and maybe survival).

Anyhow, some of the youth accepted the values and attitudes of their parents and grandparents and tried, vainly, it turns out, to conform to tradition.

Others, perhaps the majority, were selective on what values to accept as they're own and which values to ignore. This group had the most difficult time because the selection list varied with time and the changing events. They were also the most ambivalent, the most confused and the most hesitant about accepting change. They also were the most experimental. That is, they tried some stuff and found that some new behavior, look or attitudes didn't fit their personality and they discarded it, only to try something else. That may sound like a contradiction, but that is the nature of youth and of humans as a species. Contradictions abound in us and we do weird things.

The majority of this group also went to school, became employed, started businesses, went to war, went into politics and generally kept the "system" on track. Some of the men had long hair, some didn't; most, of both genders, tried weed and eventually gave it up, some didn't (both counts); most participated in the fight for civil rights – race and female – some didn't; some joined the "Youth Crusade" to elect George McGovern, too many didn't and a bunch (over 160,000) joined the peace corps.

The third group, a decided minority but also the most vocal, wanted to burn everything down and start over.

Whatever an individual's position, it was different than what had been previously been accepted. The degree of difference depended on the individual, but the fact that there was some difference was virtually universal.

OK, the stage is set. Change is about to happen. Which direction will it go?

JFK knew it and foretold of it:

"A revolution is coming – a revolution which will be peaceful if we are wise enough; compassionate if we care enough; successful if we are fortunate enough – but a revolution is coming whether we will it or not. We can affect its character; we cannot alter its inevitability."

And happen it did and the world was never the same.

The Youth Revolution!

I don't know if this particular moniker has ever been used for the 60s, if not, you heard it here first.

Use it.

Make me famous.

OK, remember thesis, antithesis and synthesis?

Here is how that comes into play:

Thesis: children are possessions. ⟶ ⟵ Antithesis: children are to be nurtured.

Synthesis: Youth is glorified.

Here's the idea. You have opposing cultural values (mores) that are essentially in conflict with one and another. The conflict rages until both entities are exhausted and new values (mores) emerge.

That is the essence of revolution. The established power structure and its *modus vivendi* (thesis) is challenged by a new or different view of how life ought to be (antithesis) and the clash results in something entirely different and usually unanticipated (synthesis). That's why a coup d'état is not a revolution although people call it that. Replacing one government with another even if the new one has a different form is not a revolution. Without changing the "hearts and minds" (where have I heard that before) of the citizenry there is no revolution.

For a revolution to occur the basic values of the community must change. It does not occur by merely replacing one government or form of government with another, it occurs because the governed have developed a different view of the established order. It is not a requirement that the system of government change, rather how people interact with their government and themselves.

The collapse of the Soviet Union is a perfect example. The Soviet system never changed the hearts and minds of the people and as soon as it collapsed the people more or less reverted back to political entities that had existed before.

In the United States, revolution can occur without changing a single part of the governing process but the revolution requires that new laws, dictates or application of existing laws be enacted to be in conformity with the people's new vision of their lives. The 19th Amendment, Brown vs. The Board of Education, Roe vs. Wade and the Miranda ruling are examples of the thesis – antithesis – synthesis (TAS) revolutionary process in action. Obviously there are thousands of other examples that have had the cumulative effect of adding, deleting or modifying the previous set mores.

Another characteristic of the revolutionary process is that it involves many issues, each with its own TAS equation but the issues are not mutually exclusive. Thus the short hair – long hair argument that resulted in "who cares" was linked by association to war sentiment, drugs, music and others.

"Does the process ever end?"

No, but it loses its immediacy, stridency and fervor as the "revolutionaries" become the new establishment and the general population becomes more comfortable with the new mores.

For example, many of the famous "Chicago Eight" became politicians, stockbrokers or whatever.

In 1968 the Democratic National convention was held in Chicago and a series of demonstrations occurred protesting the Viet Nam War and other burning issues of the day. Riots took place, some started by the police, and a whole bunch of people were arrested. Eventually eight people, dubbed the Chicago Eight, were charged with various crimes ranging from conspiracy to crossing state lines to incite riots. Eight policemen were also indicted by a Grand Jury.

The trial was a big brouhaha with a lot of antics by the defendants, a judge losing his temper and demonstrations outside the courtroom that had to be contained by the National Guard. The upshot of the whole show was that, after appeals, seven of the defendants were eventually released and charges dropped. The eighth, Bobbie Seale, spent four years in prison for contempt. That was the longest incarceration for that offence in American history.

Anyhow, Tom Hayden became a California Assemblyman, Jerry Rubin an investor and businessman, Rennie Davis became a Venture Capitalist (whatever that is), John Froines worked for OSHA and became a teacher, Bobby Seale went through a great deal of trouble after his prison term but eventually began dedicating his time to Reach! a group focusing on youth education programs. Only Abbie Hoffman and David Dellinger had trouble adjusting to the new order.

Back to the TAS thing. Some issues are not fully resolved and only a partial synthesis emerges and some individuals or small groups still cling to the thesis or antithesis side of the equation and continue to battle. The mainstream of the populace has now adapted to the new order (more or less) and has moved on while the protagonists of the old arguments become less and less relevant.

Slogans like "Family Values" and "Moral Majority" are bandied about by old guard types (regardless of age) immediately come to mind. These folks yammering about those slogans have apparently failed to notice that to the majority of Americans, the Cleavers of *Leave it to Beaver* fame don't exist anymore and haven't for some time – maybe they never did.

Marx had the idea right but he had way too much time on his hands and was generally pissed off because he couldn't get a good job so he screwed up the application. Lenin jumped on the idea and took a backward country and made it more backward. Some seventy years later the whole system took a dump.

Now we've got the Russian Mafia.

I guess progress is relative.

Back in the US of A.

Ok, the stage is set for the Youth Revolution.

The teenage monsters are loose with a lot of free time for thinking, money in their pockets, nurturing parents at their sides, hormones raging…

What to do, what to do?

Most of that seventy million young people were girls and women. They were also thinking and a few decided that the scripts outlining female roles were faulty and began writing scripts of their own. Simply put, relegation to second class was deemed to be unacceptable.

They protested, they burnt their bras, they revolutionized fashion and they demanded equality. They formed organizations and expanded on existing ones; they turned out to vote and elected people, men and women, sympathetic to their plight and there were lawsuits by the ton.

All good and the "playing field" was leveled somewhat.

But they didn't understand the feminine/masculine rule.

They didn't realize that in order to really, effectively change the scripts, the rule had to be attacked.

They made a dent into accepted customs and usages, but in the final analysis they did not change the hearts and minds of the people.

Women are still expected to be "feminine" and men "masculine".

In spite of this basic flaw, giant strides were made in seeking some measure of legal and social equality for women. Aside from the political and legal battles being waged, the consciousness of people was being modified. Many men were released from the pressure of being superior and began to create their own scripts. Women entered the workforce filling many jobs traditionally held by men and a new creativity and vigor began to emerge. Wealth expanded geometrically and the "western" lifestyle became the envy of the world.

Language was under scrutiny. Certain words and combination of words were deemed to be improper. Excellent approach because, as I mentioned before, we react to the reality we experience based on the words we use to describe it.

A conscious effort was being mounted to remove the appendage of "man" from almost all work related titles that tended to imply that only men were suited for that title. A side effect of this political correctness related to words was the slow devolvement into the abandonment of disparaging words to describe ethno-cultural "them" sub groupings. Words like nigger, honkie, spick, mick, etc have, at long last, fallen into disuse. The word nigger is experiencing some resurgence within some entertainment circles, but the resurgence is primarily financially motivated because of the shock value. I suspect that a majority of people younger than twenty-five have not heard of the other words and if they have, don't relate to their previous connotation.

Along with improvements in status came the expansion of choices and redistribution of money. The Moguls could see that a bunch of the teenagers were girls, girls also had money, let's get that money.

By now you know what I'm *not* going to do: take a conventional view of history. That's boring and no fun at all. Besides, historians are always selective in their interpretation of events, so why should they have all the fun?

I'd love to resurrect Igor, but things are much too confusing by now for old Igor, so I'm stuck with selecting a few events that I perceive as having affected a woman's view of herself.

Will what I am about to say be correct?

Hell, I don't know.

You decide.

Back to what to do, what to do.

Hanging out on the corner or in the soda shop was OK but not enough. The kids were ripe for the picking.

1953 – Hugh Hefner launches *Playboy*.

Hefner was one of the new Moguls. A new product for a market that didn't exist.

Man, did he guess right!

One year no market, the next year a market so large he had difficulty keeping up with the demand.

Suddenly there was a magazine being sold at the drugstore counter that glorified women and an urbane hedonistic lifestyle.

"Glorified women? You have got to be kidding!"

I knew that would get someone's attention

Everything is relative and relative to how women were viewed pre-*Playboy,* his presentation was a step up. Everything about the magazine was slick and upscale and it preached that the established Protestant Ethic was repressive and almost evil. The magazine had an aura of intellectuality about it and you can argue that it was hype but hardly anyone saw it that way.

Yes it contained pictures of naked women but they were presented in such a way that there seemed to be a purity to them, a wholesomeness, if you will, that belied the fact that they were naked.

Good trick and Hefner pulled it off and made a pile of money.

Regardless of what you may think. The perception of what makes a woman beautiful was changed forever.

As Haldeman of Watergate fame was to say later:

"Once the toothpaste is out of the tube, it's hard to get it back in."

The magazine also pimped the idea that the act of sex was fun and good and rewarding in and of itself.

Not the first guy to say that but the first with a slick magazine that communicated that message every month to millions of readers.

"What about the teenage girls and women of the time?"

I don't know for sure, but they didn't rise in protest although there was some of that by men. It is fair to assume, however, that there was a certain amount of comparative anatomy going on behind closed doors.

The effect of *Playboy's* sex is good, sex is fun may have had a tangential effect on girls but it sure did bring up a lot of discussion.

Not with the parents, among teenagers.

Tah, Dahh!

The first TAS: Thesis – Modesty is good; Antithesis – Sexy is better; Synthesis: Total confusion. Not really, but think of all the corollaries: sexy = more sex; more sex = higher risk of pregnancy…you can see where this is going.

Anyhow, teenage girls, much to their male parent's consternation, were fascinated by the idea of being sexy.

New values were being formulated. Actually formulated is not a good word because it of implies some sort of rationale and conclusion, perhaps posed or just thought about is a better descriptor. Some precedent existed for questioning sexual mores in the writings and actions of the "Lost Generation" of the twenties and thirties and the "Beat Generation" of the late forties and fifties, but they never had the marketing skill of *Playboy*. Neither one of these groups were "generations" at all. Rather they were an amalgam of artists (writers, painters, musicians, etc.) who, particularly the beats, glorified non-conformity (the term beatnik was first coined in 1958 as a combination of "beat" and "sputnik").

Many of the mothers of the teenagers of the fifties were born in the twenties, had lived through the Depression and worked during the War. Many took vicarious pleasure in seeing their daughters "have good times". They didn't encourage sex, although some might have, but they encouraged an active social life. The mothers promoted parties, slumber parties, proms, and other activities with the unwritten and unsaid idea of having a good time while you can – implying that when the girls got married, the "good times" would end.

Sound familiar?

The mothers encouraged makeup, trendy fashions, hair styling and all sorts of accoutrements to make their daughters the "belles of the ball".

Where have I heard that before?

Cinderella anyone?

Not to be outdone by *Playboy,* magazines catering to teenage girls hit the stands and sold like hot cakes.

1953 – *The Wild One*. Bad boy Marlon Brando comes to the silver screen and scares the hell out of everyone over thirty. The boys loved it and the girls were "all a flutter".

My compadres and I saw the film and picked up on all sorts of symbolism. Johnny (Marlon Brando) was angry. It's not clear what he was angry at but we decided that he was angry with his parents and a system that wouldn't listen to him. Of course we weren't that angry, but sullenness among teenage boys became cool and speaking to one's parents in grunts, like Brando, became almost a requirement.

My father tolerated that crap, but there were clearly defined lines and should I cross them, I knew with absolute certainty that my life as I knew it would cease to exist.

The monsters were starting to ooze out. Teenagers had begun to bite the hand that fed them, a practice that continues today and is accepted as normal.

Why? I have no clue.

Anyhow, bad boys become the rage among teenage girls.

Brillcream, Duck-tail haircuts, black leather jackets and Levi's became de rigor.

There wasn't a lot of boinking yet but a hell of a lot of base stealing.

1955 – *Rebel Without a Cause*. Holy cow! A movie about the dysfunctional relationship between parents their children, particularly children being raised without a father figure and how the kids felt about that. At that time divorce was still somewhat of a stigma but we all knew of kids whose parents had divorced, but that wasn't the issue. The issue was that dads were not role models. Nobody wanted to be like his or her dad. He worked all the time, he got no respect and he was always called upon for discipline.

Wait until your father gets home.

Teenagers across the country identified with the angst portrayed by the protagonists of the film.

For the girls: Jimmy Dean. Sultry, sexy, misunderstood and on fire!

1955 – *Blackboard Jungle.* A little social consciousness thrown in for good measure. A movie about a classroom just like yours, or so you imagined, where we yearned for an understanding, strong, sensitive teacher.

I believe that it was also the first sound track, *Rock Around the Clock* by Bill Haley and the Comets, to produce a hit single. It sold 25 million copies.

1955 – Elvis. Now the parents were really losing control but they desperately hung on.

1956 – *And God Created Woman* staring Brigitte Bardot. Dumb film but she pranced around in a bikini.

The suit took California by storm and by 1960 it was considered THE suit to wear at the beach. Bryan Hyland recorded the hit song: *Itsy Bitsy Teeny Weeny Yellow Polka dot Bikini*, and later the heroine of the *Mickey Mouse Club* starred in the famous beach party films.

Synthesis: Bikini accepted (four years).

1959 – Barbie was introduced and in the first year sold about 350,000 dolls. Couple that with Disney's *Cinderella* and you've got a lot of girls pretending. Some would say imagining, but in my mind the jury is still out on that one.

Bad stuff?

Absolutely not!

Girls, also no longer possessions, were experimenting with new ideas and a new consciousness of self.

1960 – Birth Control pills. The sexual revolution was off and running.

1962 – The Beatles. Long hair was definitely in!

1963 – *The Feminine Mystique.* Betty Friedan's book about how women were literally getting screwed.

Ms. Friedan apparently polled her classmates who had graduated from Smith College in 1942 and from the data she hypothesized that women were *victims* of a false *belief system* that insists that her only identity and meaning to her life can be found in husband and family.

What better way to foster insecurity than to declare that you under the power of something as intangible as "belief system"?

Let me see.

By definition a woman is a victim and therefore is acted upon by forces outside herself over which she has no control.

Now that's positive.

NOT!

The thing that victimizes you is a "belief system".

To stop being a victim you must neutralize/eliminate/destroy the "belief system".

Belief system. Now there's a good one. It sounds like words taken from a psychiatrist's of psychologist's buzzword generator. You know, 6,3 (sixth word from column one and third word from column two) or some such thing.

be·lief *n.* Something accepted as true; especially a particular tenet, or body of tenets, accepted by a person or group of persons.

sys·tem *n.* A group of interacting, interrelated or interdependent elements forming or regarded as forming a collective entity.

Ok, we've got a noun acting like an adjective on something that is a "collective entity". How can a word like belief, a noun, be used to describe (tell what it is, is like) anything?

A belief pole?

More to the point, a belief collective entity.

An electrical (adj.) system (n.) works. The word electrical tells what kind of collective entity the thing is.

Belief system: nonsense.

Jeez, no wonder we can't communicate. Why not use a word like tenet or mores, which is really what is being talked about?

ten·et *n.* An opinion, doctrine, principle or dogma held by a person, persons or organization.

mo·res *pl., n.* The accepted traditional customs and usages of particular social group that comes to be regarded as essential to its survival and welfare, thence often becoming, through general observance, part of a formalized legal code.

There you have it. Igor and his descendants regarded breeding as essential to their survival and made up customs or laws to assure that women were available for that function.

Mores. Pretty straight forward to me, so what's with "belief system"?

I have no idea except to note the obvious which is: there's a bunch of "experts" out there pretending that they know something and since they don't really, they invent combinations of words to confuse people and since the people don't really know what the "experts" said, the people assume that the "experts" know something.

Perfect. Argumentative circularity at its best.

It's been more than forty years since I read Ms. Friedan's book so I can't remember whether she used the terminology "belief system" in its current connotation or not (I suspect that she didn't), but what she basically said is: Ladies, you are being treated like dog poo, get mad and don't take it anymore!

Right on!

Unfortunately a bunch of people jumped on the image of woman being a victim and the image that women are innately insecure was created.

So how does one neutralize/eliminate/destroy mores?

Revolution comes to mind.

Thesis: A woman should be kept barefoot, pregnant, raise the children and care for her man, i.e., Family Values.

Antithesis: A woman can buy all the shoes she wants; is not just a life support system for a womb; universal childcare and the man has to do the vacuuming.

Synthesis: Men are Pigs.

Not exactly the expected result and a little petulant, but a generally universal held belief by Americans of the female persuasion.

In spite Ms. Friedan and NOW's best efforts, a substantial number of young girls felt that being sexy was a good thing and....

1965 – Mary Quant (new Mogul) introduces the mini skirt. In a year the market drops about 300 points (same amount as the Depression). Again many learned economists have all kinds of theories about why the crash happened and again they were wrong. This time, however, a recession was averted because the teenagers were snatching up the new fashions, and related stuff, faster than it could be put on the racks – mostly from companies that weren't listed on the Stock Exchange.

1966 – Twiggy. The first supermodel and she was modeling all the latest and greatest teen fashions.

The end of reason.

Suddenly skinny was cool and a requirement.

The thirteen year olds of 1953 are now twenty-six and are wondering if they are missing the fun.

In ten short years, a whole bunch of girls had gone from training to be a wife to burning their bras.

The Moguls discovered that sexiness sells products and suddenly, big tits, shapely legs, skinny women and all that stuff was/is all over the place.

The birth of the Feminine Industrial Complex.

What had happened to little girl's minds?

- They had gone through several millennia of being told that they were worthless or at best second-class.
- *Playboy* – redefines beauty.
- Cinderella and Barbie – you are what you look like.
- *Feminine Mystique* – women are victims of a system.
- Twiggy – thin is in and normal weight is passé.

The Moguls, actually New Moguls by now, were sucking up every possible penny they could from the teenage market, the youth market and the wanabee young market.

Along comes the credit card. In 1950, Diners Club issued the first credit card and met with huge success. By the end of the 1960s every major store had its own card and by the 1970s they had become a requirement. The Moguls had figured out how to triple or quadruple the spending power of their focus markets.

A new image had been created.

Youth is good, youth is attractive, young is what we want to be. "Fifty is the new thirty!" exclaim the medical Moguls, the cruise ship Moguls, the fashion Moguls, the car Moguls and just about any other Mogul we can think of.

They want your dough and it is essential that the rule of masculine/feminine remain intact.

Male = virile, strong, etc. Female = attractive, homemaker, pliant, etc. Sells a lot of stuff.

Although some of the changes in our social behavior caused by The Youth Revolution will have a lasting effect, the reality is that fawning at the idol of youth probably won't.

Events have occurred and are occurring that will have unintended consequences and opportunities.

The Baby Boomers are aging.

The children of the fifties and sixties, Baby Boomers, are now older but apparently they had such a good time they want to stay young.

Obviously that is impossible but the cultural pressures are almost impossible to resist and the desire to *appear* young seems to hit women harder than men.

During the two decades (1960 to 1980) of revolution, many entwined syntheses began to emerge that produced a new culture. One of the unforeseen syntheses of The Youth Revolution (TYR) has been a shift in the behavior towards and the perception (thought) of the value of a significant portion of the population. The revolution replaced the thought characteristic that venerated age with the thought that age is weak, less utile and possibly a burden on the society.

The perception used to be, less than one hundred years ago, that the older members of society were imbued with wisdom and knowledge that could only be obtained through longevity. Now they can't work the DVR and don't own smart phones and hence are somehow quaint.

"Dad, I've told you a thousand times that the TV doesn't have to be on for the DVR to record."

That thinking changed the community's behavior towards issues of status and worth. Prior to TYR, an individual's status within the community was defined in terms of wealth, power and property, all of which were generally associated with age. Post TYR the definition of status became more fluid and considerably less tangible.

Playboy and similar magazines (catering to both genders) as well as advertising began creating an image that youth and hedonism are "good" while age and restraint is "not-so-good".

Naturally the 15 to 30 crowd lapped it up and because of their slurping, the Moguls jumped in with both feet and reinvented the meaning of status.

Status became synonymous with owning things. Not necessary things, but excessive things. Status became superficial rather than substantive.

A new phrase was invented: status symbol.

The phrase was first coined in 1955 but was popularized in Vance Packard's book *The Status Seekers,* published in 1959.

Available credit flourished and suddenly people who showed financial restraint had less status because they didn't surround themselves with the requisite symbols.

Flashy cars, flashy house, flashy spouse, flashy children became a requirement for status.

Example: a Cadillac used to be an old person's car and it symbolized wealth and status. Now, circa 2005, a Cadillac Escalade is cool and marketed to the younger crowd with too much financial credit.

Of course none of the images portrayed in the advertising were/are true or even remotely accurate but no matter, the 15 to 30 crowd bought it, loved it and spent themselves into one trillion plus debt.

That crowd is now 40 to 60 and shows no signs of slowing their profligate ways and they have passed that spending culture on to their children.

Good? Nope.

Bad? Nope.

It just is.

There are some signs that the jig might be up.

Other than the current meltdown caused almost exclusively by greed, larceny, stupidity and total mismanagement, two of the most tangible signs are the Social Security System and Health Care.

Back in the day, when people became too feeble to work they were either cared for by their family or died. Social Security was invented during the Depression years to provide a minimal income for people who became too old to work, a safety net if you will. The moneys garnished from the workers and employers would only be available at a specific age. The age selected was sixty-five because, in the 1930s, that was slightly older than the general life expectancy for an individual.

Seemed like a pretty good idea. Shouldn't be too expensive because most people didn't live past sixty-five and it would help to partially remove the incentive to "save for their old age" and free up some moneys to fuel the economy.

Worked like a charm. Pretty soon the system became an integral element of the economic and political fabric of the society. The political Moguls used the system as a vote getting vehicle by expanding it and took pride in the attitude of "look what your government does for you".

In the short span of two generations, 60 years, it became apparent that most people are going to live way past sixty-five and the bite out of the worker's paycheck became larger and larger to finance the added benefits and the expected debt.

Suddenly Social Security was no longer largesse but an enormous burden and those pesky old people (over 65) are the problem. In fact, the percentage of over 65 folks in the United States has more than doubled from about 5% in the 1930s to about 12% of the total population in 2004. The actual numbers are worse because in the thirties there were about 5 million people over 65, now there are 22 million or four times as many folks while the 18 to 64 crowd has not quite doubled.

Major burden.

Healthcare has undergone a similar shift. In the thirties and forties, healthcare (it wasn't called that) primarily dealt with the treatment and, hopefully, the cure of illness. Individuals used their doctor only when they were sick and grandma's herb tea didn't work. Employers bowed to union pressures, government sanctions and a very real labor shortage and began offering health insurance, paid vacations, life insurance and other goodies as part of the employee's "benefit package".

Time passed and suddenly the whole concept of the purpose of medical services changed from solely dealing with illness to prolonging one's life through attempting to delay or minimize the natural decay of the body's systems. The primary thrust of this effort is through drugs – lots of drugs - and the abstinence of "vices".

Healthcare was invented.

Good stuff but expensive.

Logic would tell us that if the general population is less prone to disease (healthier), and it is, then the costs of maintaining that health would be less expensive.

Wrong, just the opposite is the case.

Why?

Just like a car, the costs to maintain the vehicle increase over time until those costs become prohibitive and the car is replaced. Those costs include general maintenance and replacement of worn out parts as well as accident repair.

People are the same way, except that an individual is irreplaceable.

Look at it this way, by the time a person is sixty, his/her heart has beaten almost two billion times and knees have been flexed, fingers have grasped, immune system has been exercised and brain synopses have transmitted a bunch of times.

Gotta be getting worn, don't you think and, like a mechanical part, the cost of repairing an older part is more expensive. Add to that the fact that a significant proportion of the population is living longer and that segment *expects and demands* that all the parts be kept in working order.

The costs for those services are substantial.

Again, the numbers tell the story: 1930s, 23 million people over 45; 2004, 65 million people; nearly three times as many.

That's a lot of people demanding services.

OK, so there are a lot more "older" people and the cost to supply them with what they demand is getting more expensive by the minute.

So what?

Can I assume that at some time those costs may become prohibitive and the society may decide that the diversion of resources to keep people alive beyond some "useful" time is jeopardizing its survival or at least its "standard of living"?

Yup, already is.

When that happens will the mores shift in some yet undetermined direction?

Yup.

The prime directive for our species and all other species is to survive and when conditions change, the species either adapts or perishes. The way that humans adapt is by changing the rules of conduct – our mores. In

Igor's time it was OK to dump the feeble, the infirm and the "incorrect"; now…not so much.

Now days, we strut about and claim that one of the things that makes us "superior" to other animals is that we hold each individual's life as sacred. Of course we have all sorts of exceptions to that code like: war, self-defense, the death penalty, irreparable body damage, etc.

The code and the exceptions to it are not "laws of nature" like gravity or magnetism, we made them up and we change them as conditions change and you can bet your bippy that we'll change them again when we decide that our survival is at stake.

Will the changes be better?

Depends on what you mean by "better" but they certainly will be different.

Thesis: Each individual's life is sacred.

Antithesis: Costs are prohibitive.

Synthesis: Don't know.

Some places allow assisted suicide.

Hmmm.

Do not resuscitate (DNR) instructions to medical personnel are becoming commonplace.

Hmmm.

Many companies are downgrading pensions and minimizing health care options.

Hmmm.

Maybe if I thought that being too old would mean that I was going to be set out on a flat rock and be eaten by wolves, I would try and stay young as well.

It won't work and don't worry.

There are many signs that the Youth Revolution has run its course.

Not as many young people for one thing and eventually we remember that being young generally sucked. We remember acne, angst, awkwardness, social pressure, etc. and that none of us had any brains or common sense.

It takes a long time and thousands of mistakes to develop character. The kind of character that allows us to survive economic swings, climate change, death, destruction, prejudice, lost love, etc., etc. and still have the strength to get up each day and battle the dragons with a measure of optimism and good humor.

Get up in the morning and look in the mirror. Look at the small hints of wrinkles and glory in them. They are the medals you have earned by surviving countless internal and external battles. They signify the lessons you have learned to make you stronger, more resilient and more content.

Not physically as strong as you used to be?

Who cares? That's why we have tools and you can make some teenager carry it for you.

Nine

The Femina Sapiens

When Ms. Friedan wrote about "the problem that has no name" in 1963, the collective social consciousness about a woman's position in society was beginning to evolve and new scripts were being developed creating new roles. Options other than marriage and motherhood were beginning to be demanded and since the demand was heard the options became available. Over time equality was partially established in the workplace and other areas as decreed by laws and new mores were developed. As a result how we live and think has been changed forever.

The options women demanded were not only careers but also control of her destiny. Marriage and children no longer became the be-all-end-all of a woman's life. Proof of that is that more than half of the women in the U.S. now live without a spouse.

Whoa! Back up. More than half of the women in the U.S. now live without a spouse?

What's going on here?

For one thing, the sentence should read that more than half of the adult *people* in the U.S. are living without a spouse – men and women.

Further, that fact is an indicator that marriage is not the be-all-end-all for men either.

Is there a problem?

Don't know. Probably not, except that there are a bunch of kids growing up in single parent homes.

Is there a problem?

Again, don't know.

I suppose that some people consider this state of affairs a problem and will spend countless hours researching, studying and conclusion making.

Me, I'm a simple kind of guy and I view that piece of data as proof that the society is evolving and adapting to new conditions.

Here's the deal. About fifty years ago a bunch of **Wo/man** decided that the way things were was a load of crap and weren't going to put up with it anymore. They decided that girls should be educated, get any job they want, enjoy any sport they choose, etc. and challenged the feminine side of the rule thereby writing a whole bunch of new scripts for a whole bunch of new roles.

Unfortunately no one told the guys anything except that they are pigs.

Everyone stayed with the "boys will be boys" thing.

Suddenly the boy is no longer a boy and, as a man, he can see that the social landscape is different than he had been taught. Very few new scripts and the rule, for him, remains unchallenged. He still believes that aggression, analysis, dominance, risk taking, etc. are the purview of the male and good things while compassion, affection, sympathy, etc are female things and not so good.

Unfortunately he is surrounded by females who are aggressive, etc., etc., and compassionate etc., etc. at the same time.

Whaaa?

Relationship crashes and burns.

A lot of head scratching by both parties.

A lot of corporate dysfunction.

A lot of older and/or conservative folks trying to hold on.

Too bad, the ship has left the dock – it's still in sight, but sailing never the less.

The question is then, why can't men be aggressive, etc., etc., and compassionate etc., etc. at the same time?

The answer is we can, we just need some instruction.

Somehow, at the beginning when our hands are reaching, we have to be taught that we, penis people, have options as well. That it's OK to be sensitive, that it's OK to be warm, yielding etc., etc., and that, in fact, big boys do cry.

Not as requirements, but as options.

Who decides that the options are available?

Moms.

Currently there are very few options available for boy children because of the rule. When, as infants, we display some characteristic that doesn't fit the caricature most people have in their heads as to how a boy should behave, we are corrected, gently perhaps but corrected nonetheless. Soon we learn that our infantile efforts to express ourselves are not met with the response we expect and take the easy path and stop expression altogether.

For some boys, the lack of positive feedback to their attempts at expression leads to hostility and aggressive behavior which is rewarded if the aggression stays within certain limits. Other boys shut down and still others feel comfortable with the whole arrangement.

There are probably as many combinations and nuances between comfort, shutting down and aggression that will apply to each boy child as there are children, but in the majority of cases "manly" behavior is rewarded and less manly behavior is discouraged.

As the boy child grows and begins interfacing with his peers, "manly" behavior is further reinforced. Penalties for displaying almost any "female" characteristic can be harsh indeed.

Homophobia begins. Sexual aggression is prized. Boys recount and brag about their "conquests". Of course there is a certain amount of lying involved, but no one notices or cares.

Eventually the boy matures and tries, mostly unsuccessfully, to rid himself of his programming, but there is no one to guide him so he lives something of a double life.

Relationships fail.

Kind of a mess, don't you think?

If you think I am exaggerating, just look around.

Men are generally running the show and wars are a permanent fixture; millions are starving; general health is better but the threat of disease, serious disease, seems to be lurking around the corner; solutions to crime seem to be nonexistent or the level might be increasing if you include terrorism as a crime and many millions do not have the opportunity for employment beyond subsistence level.

We still cling to ancient primordial customs that have us believe that anyone that looks different, talks differently, smells differently and at a higher level has a different government, religion or basic customs are not to be trusted.

We still cling to ancient primordial customs that prize territoriality. You know, 'hood, turf, city, state and nation.

We are desperate without possessions, human or otherwise.

The list goes on and I'll bet that you can think of several more customs that we cling to that are a direct result of manly behavior. Customs that may have been necessary for our survival and welfare back in Igor's time but now have become archaic, dangerous and stupid.

How come we can build magnificent buildings, roads, airplanes, etc and yet behave little differently than when we were foraging for food in the savannahs back in Igor's time?

How come we can compassionately send millions of dollars to assist people in distant lands who are in dire need, yet want to build a wall to keep intruders out of our turf?

How come we love all children but distain that same child as an adult because of the color of their skin or the God they worship?

How come we can own more things than we could possibly use yet lust for more?

The answer is, of course, that in spite of our tremendous intellect and material inventiveness we have not changed our mores.

They have not changed because there has been no need. Until just recently, ± a couple of hundred years, our leaders, political, economic, educational, religious, spiritual, theological, philosophical, etc. believed that the system in place was working fine and have resisted change, in spite of growing evidence that something is amiss.

Those leaders have been men inculcated with the belief that "manly" behavioral characteristics should be emphasized to the detriment of "female" traits.

Along come guys like Gandhi and Martin Luther King and throw a monkey wrench in the whole system. They say don't be aggressive, be compassionate, be soft spoken, be sensitive, be understanding etc., etc. and they revolutionize the world. A couple of thousand years ago, other guys like Jesus, Mohammed, Buddha, Confucius, etc. spread the same message and also revolutionized the world.

Hundreds of women from Elizabeth Cady Stanton and Susan B. Anthony to Friedan, Sanger and Steinem preached, cajoled, arm twisted and fought legal battles to provide inclusion of over half of the population into the decision making process and most of the world has the potential to be an infinitely better place because of their efforts.

You would think we'd get the message by now.

Apparently not.

The problem is that we still cling to the rule. We still believe that "manly" behavioral characteristics should be emphasized to the detriment of "female" traits.

"That's boloney!" You may say. "I've got a female boss and she's a tyrant."

That's because the only behavior models in the business world were created by aggressive men and to "succeed" she has to emulate them.

Also she, that individual, may just be a jerk.

Jerkdom is pretty much independent of gender.

Historians will probably disagree, but I maintain that women direct the impetus for all social change. Not necessarily political or economic change, the changes that effect how we behave.

I'm sure that thousands of examples will be offered to "prove" that my statement is incorrect but their proofs will be vacuous because prior to the fifteenth century there is no data. There are no records of what the wives, daughters or mistresses did, said, influenced, encouraged or discouraged the shakers and movers (men) of the world.

Who knows?

We do know, however, that when women finally distanced themselves from the male oppression established by the prehistoric error and started demanding some measure of parity, the social fabric of the United States and most of the industrialized world has been radically altered.

Social structures are complicated things encompassing many elements including, but not limited to, laws, economics, arts, literature, language, institutions and customs. A lot of stuff, but a social structure can be characterized by how the members of a particular society interact with one another. The type and style of interaction is determined by the human members of the society through the collective agreement of ideas. That is, human societies have philosophies and place value on its member's interaction. Thus some behavior is deemed socially appropriate and other behavior is deemed inappropriate.

Within simple societies, a family for instance, the range of accepted behavior might be limited but as membership grows the society becomes more complex and more latitude is permitted particularly if the behavior occurs outside the familial society.

There is considerable discussion as to whether the philosophies contained within the family unit determines the social tone of the society at large or is the converse more accurate

Doesn't matter.

If one were to think of society as an organism, one could say that the social organism today is a different species that it was one hundred years ago. Complicated to be sure and comprising many breeds, each with its own personality, but a new social species nevertheless. There is still evidence of sub-sets of the old social species but, as is the nature of the evolutionary process, they will either adapt or eventually become extinct.

Adaptation is the key to the survival of any species. Environmental conditions are always in flux and while some species are able to survive extreme changes, humans are considerably more fragile and require their intellect, compassion and cooperation to adapt when nature throws a curve. The new social species, comprised of humans and reflective of its components, is also fragile and thus, should external conditions change, it must adapt or sink into chaos or possibly extinction.

The question is: should we wait and see how things evolve or should we be proactive and consciously modify the social species in preparation of the environmental change?

Should you agree with me that we must start now to change our ways, let me reassure you that the foundation is already in place. What is needed now is some fine-tuning and the tuning must and will be directed by women.

I know I am repeating myself, but it needs to be said again and again until it sinks in. Women comprise more than half of the human population. That is an enormous amount of brainpower that is currently underutilized. Further, women are the primary definers, protectors and purveyors of the mores of society and thus have the power to transform how society behaves.

So, what should women do?

The first thing is to take a close look at what it means to be feminine.

From a biological point of view, we all know that women are designed to give birth and provide nutrition to a young human but that part of femininity is not unique because almost all female mammals are built with those capabilities. The thing that distinguishes the Femina[2] sapiens from the other mammals as well as the Homo sapiens is her brain[3].

There are many studies about the operation and configuration of Femina sapiens' brains and these studies are just beginning, but it has become apparent that the Femina sapiens has a brain that is designed for enhanced communication (quality not quantity) and more accurate comprehension of emotional stimuli. That means that a woman has more brain space available for verbal communication and can more accurately discern and comprehend nonverbal communication than the rest of the species.

Huge, and I mean huge, advantage for all the people out there.

Here's the deal. Since women are biologically endowed with the ability to understand verbal and nonverbal communication very acutely, have a higher sense of empathy and have a more intuitive understanding of vitality (the essence of life) they can be compassionate, nurturing and sensitive naturally and with ease. Add to that intelligence, drive, ambition, etc. and the result is femininity.

Femininity has nothing whatever to do with adornment it has to do with the innate construction of a woman's brain and all of the unique functions it performs.

Her body…well, her body is whatever it is or whatever she chooses it to be.

We live in a world dominated by hundreds of human civilizations and the ones that are successful, e.g.: provide an optimum amount of security

---

[2]   The term Homo sapiens is a male generated taxonomical term. I like Femina when used in reference to women of our species.

[3]   I am not going to reference all the research on this subject. You can find out on your own, besides this is not a rigid scientific dissertation and detailed references are not required.

and wellbeing to its members, are the result of feminine women, not girly girls, partnering with men to make it happen. No partnering or women are oppressed – no success.

This statement should be obvious to even the most casual observer because the males of our species are constantly posturing about and challenging each other to some kind of confrontation and the females have to follow around and pick up the pieces to keep civilization on track.

The optimum is when both partners have parity and the confrontations are contained. Containment doesn't mean defenseless, it means it means less aggression.

Femininity means realizing and using the unique abilities that Femina sapiens have and that they are not a subset of Homo sapiens. Femininity means taking responsibility for your body and brain whatever it is. Femininity means the power of optimism, the skill of flexibility, the power of awareness and the thrill of creativity.

Femininity has nothing whatever to do with adornment except when the process of adornment demonstrates who you are and what you are doing at that particular moment.

You are unique so show it off.

You messed up? Screw it and try again.

The power of your unique Femina sapiens brain can now tackle and solve almost any problem.

Should the concept of wealth be solely defined in terms of things one owns or by something else?

Femina will decide.

Should we continue to pathetically rely on visual physical differences to determine our interaction with others?

Women will decide.

Should the value of a working individual be determined by their position in the hierarchy?

Etc.

If you are reading this with any interest, you probably are expecting me to give you specifics on how we should behave and how we can get there.

Not going to do that.

First, I'm not a woman and thus I don't have the same knowledge of life. I understand life at level three while most women understand life at level four or higher. As a result, thinking, sensitive women can envision techniques and goals that I can't imagine.

Second. The ball is in your court. We screwed things up and are incapable of fixing it – you do it!

I will, however, offer some food for thought.

First of all, think about words. Those pesky, vaguely defined words that quite possibly are at the root of our problems.

Remember, we define our lives and most of our actions not by what we see and sense but by how we describe what we see and sense.

Here are six that are connotatively male: strong, analytical, decisive, independent, leader and aggressive. Manly words. Words that imply maleness.

The antonyms (more or less) of these words are: gentle, emotional, yielding, compassionate, tender and sympathetic. Female words. Words that imply femininity.

Right away you can see the problem because those manly words are descriptors of traits that are admired while the others, not so much. This is very unfortunate because admiration of those manly traits and the desire by individuals to be and act as those words imply is what gets us into trouble. Back in Igor's time, those traits *may* (emphasis on may) have been important for survival but today they are archaic and possibly dangerous.

Let's take them one at a time, bearing in mind that some of these attributes overlap a bit.

<u>Strong</u>

We all know what strong means and it means a lot of things but as it relates to humans there are two basic definitions: having great physical power and having a compelling personality as in being capable of the exercise of authority.

Physical strength was probably important if you were a knight running around in a lot of armor or fighting a wild animal like Tarzan or something, but today physical strength is only important in very limited occupations, such as athletes or maybe a dock worker.

A stockbroker? No.

Today, being physically fit is far, far more important to an individual's ability to survive than strength alone, thus being physically strong is O.K. but generally a big ho-hum.

That leaves a compelling personality.

A compelling personality implies leadership, the ability to direct and control other people whether through persuasiveness or charisma. It implies power and power implies mastery over the environment, ourselves and other people.

Everyone has power. You have the power to say yes or to say no; you have the power to go to work in the morning or not; you have the power to be angry or not; you have the power to be compassionate or not; etc. Even though we all have power over many things in our daily lives, most of us have limited power over other people. You may be some kind of boss, but the power you possess in that situation is derived from the hierarchy in which you work and is granted to you by the structure of the organization. It is not inherent.

In addition, the vast majority of us exercise whatever power we have with restraint and prudence. Parents, for instance, have power over their children but almost invariably temper that power with compassion, empathy and love. Some of us go nuts every once and a while but that is usually a temporary aberration. Most of us view strength of character and the power derived there from as a responsibility and although we enjoy whatever adulation we may receive as a result, we try not to abuse, which is, to us ordinary folk, is one of the facets of strength of character.

We view people who lord it over others as jerks.

Over the millennia, modern, as opposed to tribal, societies have discovered that unchecked power is not a good thing and leads to all kinds of nastiness to be foisted on the less powerful. As a result, many societies have developed systems or laws to provide some measure of constraint on the powerful. At the most basic of levels, the statement "Pick on someone your own size" is exercised to attempt to restrain the activities of schoolyard bullies. Sometimes social pressure like that works, sometimes it doesn't, but it is clear that at some level we recognize that unrestricted power is not a good thing – except to the powerful. In the United States and many other countries, a network of laws, customs and practices (mores) have been developed to restrain unbridled power that individuals might assume. These restraints apply to presidents, government officials, religious leaders, corporate executives, managers, spouses and even children.

So we live in a dilemma: a love-hate relationship with powerful people. We like strong leaders but not too strong; we love charismatic people like celebrities and religious leaders but delight in their "fall from grace"; we admire scions of industry or finance but we are convinced that they are somehow ripping us off; etc.

If what I have said about this dichotomy is true or close to it, don't you think we ought to do something about it?

Let's start by understanding the source of power. One of the elements of power is the control powerful people have over other people. That situation may seem to be "natural" but it is not. It is only convenient. It is convenient because all of us have lives to live and outside of our little spheres of power we want someone else to "direct traffic". We want government, we want police, we want Wall Mart, etc. We want all those things that bring direction, entertainment, and some sense of order to the universe outside our spheres so we can enjoy Life, Liberty and the Pursuit of Happiness.

A whole bunch of other people has to make that happen.

That bunch of other people who we call powerful is also something of an annoyance because it seems that the powerful don't have enough brains to restrain themselves from exercising too much power. When the powerful get too big for their britches, us ordinary folk stomp the crap out of them and send them to the guillotine.

Been happening for all of recorded history.

Unfortunately we install another bunch and the process repeats itself.

One would think that we would have figured out by now that no empire lasts forever, that military might alone is of little use and institutions built on greed will not stand.

Apparently not.

I suggest that what we need is to modify the definition of strong as it applies to character.

We could, for instance, decide that the characteristic of character that emanates power without compassion and empathy is defective and undesirable; that a "suitable" demonstration of compassion and empathy are prerequisites to the acquisition of power.

That may sound a little namby-pamby but it is not as far-fetched as it may seem.

For instance, if the recently incarcerated leaders of Enron, Adelphia, etc. had a little compassion and empathy for their employees and stockholders, they probably wouldn't have pilfered all that money; if some political leaders had a little compassion and empathy towards the people they are about to pummel, maybe we could avert some wars; if religious leaders had a little more compassion and empathy towards the people who don't understand or believe in something else, maybe there would have been less burnings at the steak; etc.

"That's baloney," you may say. "The world is filled with bad people and we have to be strong to keep them from taking our stuff."

True, but strength at the expense of empathy puts you at a serious disadvantage because you risk the possibility of underestimating the bad guys. Good generals understand their enemy and anticipate threats thereby minimizing the hazards to their own positions. Good politicians understand their opponents and know that they exist at the convenience of the people they lead, thus if they present the possibility of a more convenient life to the opponent's followers then the opponent stands the risk of losing her/his power base.

Further, as I mentioned before, we demand compassion and empathy from those of us ordinary folks who have strength of character – why not of our leaders?

I don't mean going to church or some other ritual, or pretending to have sprung from humble beginnings or surrounding yourself at appropriate moments with the spouse and kiddies, I mean a demonstrated pattern of behavior.

A demonstrated *pattern of behavior.*

Sounds to me like that's the purview of women and women can decide the what and how.

Women, should they choose, can break the cycle of manly leaders that have lead us down one path of destruction or another by modifying the definition of what strength of character means and demand compliance. In the political arena for instance, women with the power of their majority, could demand civility, accuracy, demonstrated compassion, positive rhetoric, etc. from those seeking elected office and refuse to support financially or otherwise those candidates who are unyielding and bound by ideology.

Remember that Hitler, Stalin, Senator Joseph McCarthy and many others were unyielding and bound by ideology and caused untold grief to millions of people. You may say that was then and that can't happen today.

You are wrong!

You are wrong because behavior demonstrating unyielding ideology destroys parity. Who currently has less parity? Women. Then that kind of behavior is an attack on women.

Think about it.

In the area of business and finance, powerful people are supported by a hierarchy and often have a lot of money. This is not necessarily a bad thing. The question is, what does that powerful person do with his/her money. Does she/he spend it on a lavish personal lifestyle or does he/she assists the community. Fancy car(s), houses, yachts, etc. are cool but is there a reasonable limit?

You decide.

Like I mentioned before, should you decide that she/he is unreasonable then exercise your collective financial clout and depose the SOB.

A short fifty years ago women demanded courtesy in the workplace and got it; you can also demand reasonable behavior.

Make that scion of industry or your immediate supervisor behave!

<u>Analytical</u>

Men are supposed to be analytical and women are supposed to be emotional.

What a crock! I don't know of many female programmers that get all emotional about the ones and zeros they are manipulating and I don't know too many men who are coldly analytical about their children. The difference, of course, is that there is a human element involved and we can all be thankful that women taught us that it's O.K. for men to exhibit emotions other than rage.

We probably need to work on envy, jealousy and revenge.

What the hell, one step at a time.

Being analytical is important and a good thing when dealing with things; when dealing with people we get ourselves into trouble. There is no doubt that some people are possessed by chemical or some other physiological imbalances that affects their behavior and those people need help, preferably from some type of analytical person, but most of us stumble our way through life and don't need analysis, we need compassion and empathy.

Armies, laws, great structures and even the automatic bread slicers are good and the result of intense analysis but the things that comfort us, that expand our empathy towards one and other that perpetuate our culture are art, writing, music, drama, comedy, etc., non-analytical things.

<u>Decisive</u>

By decisive, I mean unwavering, steadfast of purpose and able to make decisions and stick to them.

Sounds good.

Wrong!

Any dolt who does not change his/her mind when confronted by new data is living in a cave. When a leader does that, the results can be catastrophic.

Changing one's mind is an essential part of being a Homo or Femina sapiens. If old Igor didn't change his mind when Moms told him not to move on, we'd all be wandering around wondering what the hell is going on.

Just once, I would like to hear a candidate for political office say that they are trying to figure it out instead of weaseling and squirming and generally making fools out of themselves and dodging the issue.

Very important. New ideas and changing one's mind is essential to our survival.

<u>Independent</u>

Everybody depends on someone else.

The day of the mountain men is gone.

Get over it.

Ask directions when you are lost or stay lost.

Even so called "free thinkers" depend on what has come before.

Even old Igor knew that teamwork and cooperation was the key to survival and he wasn't too bright.

Somehow we got the idea that to be independent was a good thing. I suppose it is coupled with the strong thing because back in the day, when we were just emerging from the caves, the leaders tended to be stronger than everyone else. Important because strength was a requisite for survival and protection but even the strong guys were dependent on the tool guys, the farmer guys, the builder guys, etc. So, since everybody wants to be the boss of something, a strong character and the image of independence seemed to be the ticket.

A lot of grunting and chest pounding going on – kind of like today.

The trouble was that the leader types kept getting bumped off – kind of like today.

A lot of disorganization – kind of like today.

Along come George and Lisa. You remember them and that old black magic called love

A little organization, a little dependence and culture began to march on.

Trouble was, George was now the boss and he wasn't independent. Lisa was out of the food gathering business and she and her rug rats had to be maintained.

George was immature, probably about 20 or younger, and unhappy.

Lisa had to keep George happy in the arrangement so she could be provided for and convinced him that she belonged to him and encouraged him to do his own thing.

She taught the boy children to be strong and believe in the myth of independence and the girl children to pretend to be dependent.

Huge error, and we are still recovering from it.

Independence: a myth.

<u>Leader</u>

Leaders lead by the consent of the led. Period.

No consent? Off with his/her head.

<u>Aggressive</u>

Assertive, bold and energetic. Sounds like a good woman to me.

Trouble is, a lot of men, when confronted be a good woman like that, label her as pushy.

I don't know how to break it to you, Mr. Man or Ms Woman, but when you label a lady as pushy you are wearing your insecurity on your sleeve.

Stop being insecure, suck it up and deal with it!

'Nough said.

I'm going to give you an example of how adherence to the rule and archaic definitions hamper us from solving current problems.

Terrorism.

Up to a few decades ago, terrorism was a tool utilized by various political movements to destroy the populace's confidence that the existing social order could keep them safe. Having successfully shaken the populace's confidence, the new Moguls could step in and establish a new social order – a tool to grab power.

For instance, the IRA's goal was/is to rid Briton from Ireland, Arafat and the PLO to establish a Palestinian State and get rid of Israel, Manachem Begin and the Hagana to rid the British and found Israel, Quantrell's Raiders during the American civil war, Nathaniel Greene, etc.

Historically, terrorism has been only marginally successful and when a new social order was established the terrorists were usually disposed of.

Can't have your own guys blowing up things.

Recently, groups that profess some sort of religious justification for their actions have adopted the tool.

As usual, religious justification confuses the hell out of everybody since the goals are not clear. Are they political? Are they religious? Is the act an end in and of itself?

Not clear and probably a mixture of all three.

Because of their professed allegiance to some religious dogma, the modern terrorists can often find sanctuary and recruits within the mainstream of the populace, thus making it very difficult to root them out. Further, the modern terrorist's goal is not to win anything, it's just to not give up. That's why they blow themselves up – can't lose because you didn't kill me. Besides, I'm going to a better place.

Current anti-terror techniques rely primarily on containment and enhanced vigilance.

Not terribly successful because the terrorist's targets are only vaguely connected to the act. Also there is confusion on whether a particular act is terrorist or an act of war.

Depends on who's doing the defining.

We don't know what to do and whom to do it to.

The reason this dilemma exists is because we are ignoring the source of the problem.

The majority of modern terrorists spring from social orders that hold women in very low regard. As a result, women have little or no voice and are thus prevented from having any measurable impact on their societies.

This condition may have been a necessary for survival centuries ago but now, with mass communication available almost anywhere, the disconnect between the reality of the whole world, wherein they see women participating in activities that are in direct conflict with their set of mores, creates an untenable position. The words used to describe reality no longer conform to the reality experienced and fantasies are invented to resolve the disconnect thus creating a mass psychosis. Therefore, when a suicide bomber is blowing himself/herself and others up, he is really attempting to maintain a social order in which women are totally subservient and will regain that state when he is surrounded by a bunch of virgins. The modern terrorist's attack is against women, not politics, foreigners or anything else.

In the industrialized world, men have whined when women start to achieve parity, in other places they blow themselves up. The veil-less, hardworking, modern women of Israel must really piss these guys off.

The women in those societies have been living with the disconnect for centuries, understand it well, mourn over the condition but are powerless to make change and save their worlds. Therefore, if the impact of the modern terrorist is to be minimized, change the hearts and minds of the women in those societies. Get them to believe that they can teach their children that options are available, that parity is achievable and necessary, and that compassion, gentleness and cooperation are infinitely more valuable traits than machismo.

Thirty years or less, the problem will disappear.

Current methods? Maybe never.

Far fetched? Maybe, but think about it.

The current construct requires the huge expenditures of resources, massive armies both overt and covert, the erosion of the civil liberties of those believed to be under attack and the use of medieval methods (torture) to obtain information from individuals believed but not proven to be perpetrators. The result of all of this gets us no closer to solving the problem.

Maybe we are addressing the wrong problem.

Just a thought.

Lately, in the United States, many men and a few misguided women have begun an attack on women that also has the objective of suppression. These people trivialize women by considering them as only baby machines and are doing everything in their power to eliminate any options a woman may have. The tactic is to use the abortion and contraception boogeymen as an excuse. Several States are systematically excluding funding for Planned Parenthood because the organization, as its name suggests, counsels women on family planning and offers birth control medicine and abortion as an option. The fact that the organization provides many other services for women such as mammograms, sexually transmitted disease information for prevention, birth control information (also a no-no) and other medical information important to women is of no consequence.

This tactic is only the beginning as exemplified by the State of Wisconsin which rescinded its equal pay law because "Money is more important to men."

You see, the attack on abortion is justified by the religious definition of murder and once that is accomplished the next step is to minimize or marginalize women on all kinds of issues that are only tangentially related to religious beliefs.

Not much different than the jihadist terrorists.

Now you, everywoman, can put up with that by following all the rules or you can discard them and establish new rules that will lead us all into a better future.

There exists a comprehensive list of characteristics that people, through surveys, have attributed to be either female or male called the Bem Sex Role Inventory. Go through the list and define them in the context of this century and beyond and you may find the key to new rules.

You can decide that you are not only a life-support system for a womb; you can decide to admire yourself for who you are, not what you look like; you can embrace the fact that you are getting older; you can be proud of your own mind, your own character, your own sense of humor and not be a reflection of someone else and you can recognize the power you have by just being a woman.

You can recognize that you, woman, have been endowed with a certain genetic physiological characteristics that served to create civilization and you must acknowledge that power and regain your position as the creator, purveyor and protector of the mores of our species and you must demand that you be recognized for that most important role.

This is what this old guy sees:

- That the species made a cultural error many moons ago that has caused the species untold grief for thousands of years. That error was the removing of legal equality and social parity from the female. That error, which began a few centuries before recorded history, has been presumed to be a defining characteristic of our species and that premise is wrong.

- That women and some enlightened men, have been fighting for centuries to correct that error but on the brink of success, many women have opted for trivia, which is their right, but has caused some considerable confusion and has served to perpetuate the myth. Should we continue to support the deception created by the error then the species will suffer dire consequences in the foreseeable future and those cultures that maintain the error will be doomed to a perpetual cycle of civil unrest, poverty and possible extinction.

- The solution is obvious and the targets are the mores. Males are not the enemy. The enemy is those accepted traditional customs and usages that have come to be regarded as essential to our survival and welfare and only women can change them.

All I ask is that you, everywoman, imbue us all with your optimism, open your purses less, reject the images of who you are not, exercise you brains and save us from chaos.

The time for foolishness is done. Now that it is recognized that all of you are a power to be reckoned with, rise up and demand that we all eschew the values of the past and invent a new order wherein a person has parity simply because that person is a person.

Tough job…

But…

After all, you are strong, you are invincible, you are woman!

9 798888 945116 7